ROBERT CRANDALL

Please, Sister

Please, Sister

Robert Crandall

RobertCrandallAuthor@gmail.com

or through this website:

https://RobertCrandall.com

ISBN: **978-1-7329814-5-4**

ALSO BY ROBERT CRANDALL

Night Winds

Rose House

*God In Her Own Universe:
Beginnings*

ACKNOWLEDGMENTS

Special thanks to my wife, Mary Sue, for her support during the creation of this book and the long hours she spent on it, as well as the many other ways she adds to my life. I couldn't have completed it without her. Also, to our son, Rob, for his unflagging encouragement.

Thanks also go out to friends who reviewed and commented on this book, especially my fellow writers in the Thursday Night Novel Critique group: Betty Popp, Mark P. Bradley, Ryan Cort, Connie Mayta, Beatrice Underwood-Sweet, and Pat Wollenberg. Their contributions added greatly to the clarity and quality of this book. Special thanks to my editor, Jayne Lewis.

Any errors or omissions are exclusively mine.

Please, Sister

"What do you want from me?"
"Everything."

CHAPTER 1

A cold wind blew down the street behind him, so Jeff turned up the collar of his brown leather jacket and slipped his hands into his pockets. He had only a few more blocks to go to the bar where he was meeting his buddies, if that was the right term for them.

As he walked down the sidewalk next to the park, he watched the wind pick up a discarded candy wrapper and carry it along, only to drop it in one of the ubiquitous green metal municipal trash cans. With a grin, he crossed Park Street to be on the same side as Mario's Bar and Grill.

For a Friday night, Mario's was moderately crowded, but it was still early. *Give it a couple of hours and we wouldn't be able to find a table, or hear ourselves talk.* Looking around, he spotted his friends in a side room at a table looking out the picture glass window onto the darkened street. They would have seen him if he had come his normal way, but he had other things to do tonight and he came in from the opposite

1

side.

"Hey, Jeff, about time you got here. We were going to start looking for you," said Marcus, his old college roommate, who was unpredictable and would try to sell you anything.

"I sent you a text saying I'd be late with work stuff. Didn't you get it?"

Marcus looked at his phone. "Hmm, guess I didn't hear it in here. Too noisy."

Jeff shook his head. "Anyway, it's too cold to be out wandering around." He gave Laura a hug, and Karen—his on-and-off girlfriend—a kiss on the cheek.

"Wait, don't I get a kiss too?" Marcus asked.

Jeff raised his eyebrows at his former roommate. "You can kiss my cheek if you want, but not these," he said, shaking his head and patting his face.

"Crude! You are so crude—will you never change?" Marcus commented.

They all broke into laughter. This was normal fare for a Friday night.

Turning to Laura, Jeff asked, "Did you talk to Mom today? When I talked to her this morning, she sounded pretty bummed out about not getting the job she applied for."

"Yeah, she was, but this afternoon she heard back from The Corvette Shop. They want her to come back for a second interview, so she feels better about things."

"What would she be doing at a car place?"

"Umm, selling them? It's what she's been doing for the last fourteen years. Or did you forget?"

"She's never sold cars before. And these are used ones. Our mother might become a used car salesperson? Really?"

Laura shook her head. "Chill out, dude. She could sell refrigerators to Eskimos if she wanted to, and you know it. Think about all the stuff she talked Dad into."

Jeff rolled his eyes before looking over at Karen and asking her, "So what are we drinking tonight—or do I get to have something I like for a change?"

"Shots. But not any shots, we're doing rye whiskey tonight."

"Tell me you're joking, please," Jeff responded.

Karen grinned at him. "Nope, and we're already one ahead of you so you need to catch up."

His eyes scanned the room for a moment. "Umm, is that really necessary?"

Karen smiled at him, batting her eyelids. "Don't you want to play along?" She pursed her lips and blew him an air kiss. "Never know, you might get lucky tonight."

After a long week at work and a rough day today, the answer was no, Jeff didn't want to play along. He wondered briefly why getting lucky usually involved large quantities of alcohol, but he let it drop. Instead, he said, "Yeah, sure. Order me two of them."

"Oh, and since you're late, you have to buy," Karen added.

He frowned, shaking his head, then ordered another round of drinks for them, with two for himself, and watched the waitress saunter away, swinging her hips. Turning back to Karen he said, "So is there some kind of plan for tonight?"

Marcus looked over at him. "Well, your lovely sister has been trying to convince us to get palm readings, but I have some misgivings about this idea."

Jeff laughed, "Well, you better go along with her if you want to get lucky tonight."

Laura slapped his arm. "You are hopeless." After a brief interval, she added, "There's this place a couple of blocks away where Madame Onofre does readings. It's something I've always been curious about and it beats sitting here drinking all night."

Marcus choked on his drink. "Are you sure about that last part?"

"Yes. You're worse than Jeff. Only one thing on your mind."

Jeff shook his head. "Not really. Sometimes two."

They laughed again while the waitress delivered their drinks, rubbing her hip against Jeff in the process. As she walked away, Karen said, "Should I be jealous?"

"Why do all the girls like you better than me?" Marcus asked.

"Maybe because I'm not such an ass," Jeff said with a smirk.

"There you go again," Marcus replied. "Do I need to take you out in the alley and whup you?"

"Think you could?"

Marcus shook his head. "Well, no. I think we settled that one a long time ago."

Turning back to his sister, Jeff said, "So what brought up this idea all of a sudden?"

"It's not sudden. I've thought about it for a long time, but never got around to it. Tonight is as good as any other time."

"Okay," he continued, "I'm game. And since Marcus has ulterior motives, I'm pretty sure he'll play along. What about you, Karen?"

"Darn, out-voted again. It's a conspiracy." After a brief pause, Karen added, "Yeah, I'm in."

Jeff grabbed the first of his shots and raised it in the air. "To palm readings."

They matched him, and all downed the drinks together.

CHAPTER 2

As they walked the few blocks, the buildings shifted from commercial to old residential; the houses were tired, with peeling paint, and a few were boarded up. Jeff suspected they were getting closer to the bad side of town, but it would only be for a short while so it didn't bother him. When they got to Madam Onofre's house, an older white bungalow with dormer windows on the upper floor looking out over the porch as if they were watching, there was a lit sign in the window advertising 'Palm Readings – Walk-Ins Expected.' But to get to the door, there were two flights of concrete steps with painted iron pipe railings climbing the steep front lawn. Marcus complained about it, but Laura just shook her head when he did and started running up the stairs ahead of him.

"Show-off," Marcus grumbled.

"Maybe you should run with me in the mornings. Might do you good."

He huffed and frowned at her as they got to the door and went in.

The front room was over-furnished with too much 'stuff' sitting around for Jeff's taste, but it didn't surprise him: oriental rugs, lighted candles including one of the pink Himalayan salt candles, decks of tarot

7

cards and numerous copies of *Today's Psychic* for customers to browse. The large opening to the other parts of the house was curtained off so there was nothing else they could see. Soft Eastern-styled music played in the background.

From the other room, a woman's pleasant voice said, "I'll take you one at a time please. Decide who goes first and come through the drapes."

Jeff glanced around, searching for a video camera but didn't see one. Probably hidden, he thought, raising one eyebrow. Still, he sat down and relaxed. What was the worst that could happen? He might even enjoy this.

Catching his breath, Marcus said, "Laura, you should probably go first since this was your idea." He paused for a moment. "If you need help, yell for me."

"I'm sure I'll be fine," she replied as she parted the curtain and went through.

With the background music and the heavy curtain, they couldn't hear anything from the other room except occasional murmurs, so the three of them sat around complaining about their day at work and speculating on what could be happening with Laura's reading.

"She's probably telling Laura she should marry me quickly, before I get away," Marcus commented.

"Or maybe she's telling her she should get away quickly before you ask her to marry you," Karen poked.

PLEASE, SISTER

"I'm starting to feel picked on here."

Jeff grinned. "I thought you were used to it by now."

That got another frown from Marcus.

Since the palm readings apparently took a while, they quieted down and Jeff started browsing through a magazine then set it aside and looked at news on his phone while Marcus and Karen complained about their individual evil bosses and what had been inflicted on them today.

After about fifteen minutes, Laura came back out through the curtain wearing a subtle smile, but saying nothing.

Marcus asked, "How did it go? Did she tell you we were going to get married and live happily ever after?"

Laura shook her head, looking at him. "As a matter of fact, no, she didn't say anything about you. But she did say we shouldn't discuss our reading with anyone else." Saying nothing more, she sat down and smiled at them.

Karen said, "Fine. I'm going next," and got up to disappear through the curtain.

Marcus looked at Jeff. "Is your sister always like this, or just with me?"

"Hmm—I'd have to say she's pretty much like this all the time. She used to pull stuff like this on me when we were younger, but I got tired of it and when she tried it, I'd get up and wander off. That would annoy her."

"Jeff…" Laura interrupted.

Her brother shrugged. "True, isn't it?"

"Don't go giving away my secrets and don't go offering suggestions like 'get up and walk away.'"

"I'm caught in the middle here, Sis. You've picked up occasional comments from me about Marcus, even back when we were in college together, so turnabout is entirely fair." He turned back to his phone again and scrolled through the news, leaving both Laura and Marcus scowling at him.

A short while later, Karen came back out, also smiling. She looked over at Jeff in particular, and grinned at him, but said nothing. He eyed her warily.

Marcus spoke up. "Enough of this, I'm going in. If I'm not back in twenty minutes, come rescue me."

Jeff raised his eyebrows. "From a palm reader?"

Marcus shrugged. "Well, you never know," and with that he disappeared through the curtain.

Karen came over and sat on the couch by Jeff, linking her arm though his and putting her head on his shoulder. He watched her out of the corner of his eye while he pretended to read, but several times she caught him looking and smiled at him. This went on until Marcus showed back up, also smiling.

"With all these smiles, I'm starting to worry," commented Jeff.

"Losing your nerve?" his sister asked.

He shook his head and went through the drape into the other room. It was darker than the front room. It took a moment for his eyes to adjust so he could see where he was going. A small, ornate table with a candle and two chairs sat near one wall, but no one else was present, so he seated himself and waited. The furnishings were much like the other room. When he considered it, he suspected this would be the dining room if it wasn't used for readings. He looked around for a moment before a young woman came through a back doorway, smiling warmly.

He forgot to stand up when she walked in the room. She was draped in a fabric gown that fell to the floor, with satin slippers peeking out from beneath it like the kind ballet dancers wear. But it was her hair that took his breath away. Covered by a scarf, flaming red curls poked out all around her face, giving the effect of an unruly halo. He could have sworn the hair was moving all by itself. All of this was complemented by her pale skin and dark eyeliner surrounding the brightest blue eyes he had ever seen.

After a moment, he remembered his manners and stood. "Sorry, you surprised me. I was expecting someone a little older."

"I'm Sister Anya, Madam Onofre's associate. We take different evenings to do readings so one of us is always available when our clients need us. I hope you don't mind." She seemed to be trying to hold back a bigger smile to be more professional, but it wasn't working very well.

"Umm, no, not at all. You're actually quite lovely, if you don't mind my saying."

She laughed. "Complimenting the reader does not make your reading come out any better." She paused and gestured to his chair, and settled across the table from him in the other one.

"So you're Jeff?"

He raised his eyebrows. "Wow, you're good."

"Well, your sister talked some about you. I'm probably not really *that* good. Let me see your palm, either hand, your choice."

He put his right hand on the table, palm up, waiting, while he watched her face and hair, mesmerized.

She settled her elbows on the table and reached across to take his hand. When they touched, a sharp electric shock ran through them both and they jumped, Jeff knocking over his chair and stumbling backwards in the process. He glanced at his hand, and back to her. "What happened?"

Looking like a frightened puppy, she backed away from the table and bumped the wall, staring at him, "Who are you? What are you?"

He shook his head. "No one special. I'm a regular guy."

Her fear was quickly replaced by anger. "No, you're not. You're lying to me." She moved behind her chair and put her hands on it to support and protect herself. Her voice was louder. "Get out of here. Don't come back, ever. Leave now."

"But what about my reading?"

Her anxiety was building. "NO! Go. I don't want to see you ever again. Don't come back here. Now leave."

He mumbled, "Sorry," and turned to go as the curtains parted and his three friends came rushing through to see what all the racket was about. "Are you okay?"

"All of you, get out of my house and don't come back again."

They turned to look at Jeff. He shrugged and led them out.

CHAPTER 3

Around noon, Jeff woke with a splitting headache. The night before, after the walk back and after assuring his friends that no, he hadn't attempted to hit on Sister Anya, the four friends had parted. Each went their own way, disturbed by the rapid turn of events and Jeff's refusal to explain what happened. As the others left, Jeff went back into Mario's and had several more drinks while trying to piece together the events at Madam Onofre's.

Now, even with the morning headache, his first thought was of The Girl, Anya. Regardless of what had happened, he wanted to see her again. No, he *needed* to see her again, soon. He knew it would not be easy. On the other hand, it was extremely important to get this right—it might be his only chance. The word obsession came to mind, but he shrugged it off. Something more fundamental was at stake for him.

Dragging himself out of bed, he headed for the shower, considering the best way to approach this.

An hour later he sat in a coffee shop where he could see the palm readers' house. From his seat in the front window, he had a clear view up the street and could almost pick out the front door. If Sister Anya came out, he would spot her, though he still had no idea what he was going to say. He considered the problem while he sipped a caramel latte that he used to wash down some ibuprofen. He had to make this work.

After three more hours and two more lattes, he was tired of pretending he was working on his laptop and he'd made no progress on his plans. In addition, he was hyped and frustrated. Shoving the laptop into his backpack, he left the cafe and walked up the street. The 'Palm Readings' light shined through the parlor window, unlike earlier when he had gone by, so he climbed the stairs and entered the house.

The voice he heard was different—definitely not The Girl. It was female, but sounded older, more confident. "Please come through the curtain."

He did so and saw a middle-aged woman in a robe much like Anya had worn but without the slippers. Instead she wore practical leather flats that were almost covered. The defining scarf covered her head, proclaiming her a mystic of some sort. "I'm Madam Onofre, please sit down."

He looked down at the floor for a moment, then back at her face. "Umm, I was hoping to see Sister Anya."

At this she looked up, startled, and rose up from her chair. "You! She told me about you. You will never see her again if I have anything to say about it, and I do. Get out of here and don't come back. I don't care what you came for. You are not welcome."

"Please, I want to talk to her. I can sit across the room or on the other side of the curtain. She can keep a door between us, I don't care. I won't hurt her."

"You don't understand what will hurt her and what won't. You have fifteen seconds to be out the door or I'll call the police." With this, she picked up the phone handset and he heard a dial tone. Shaking it at him, she added, "I can have legal action taken against you if I have to. Remember that."

Stumped and confused, Jeff shook his head and walked out the door, trying to figure out why they hated him and what he could do about it.

CHAPTER 4

The next morning found Jeff sitting in the same cafe, in the same chair, drinking another latte, still hoping to see Anya. He still hadn't come up with a plan, other than hoping Anya would be doing readings tonight so he could at least say a few words to her.

He had ignored the phone calls from his friends the prior day. Laura and Marcus had both left voice messages and texts asking if he was okay. Karen had left a message offering to come over, saying she would do anything she could to help him feel better. *Not sure what her palm reading said, but it wasn't anything like mine.*

He was finishing his coffee when one of the young women cleaning up the tables came over. "Want me to take that for you? I can get you another if you'd like—on the house." She reminded him of the waitress at Mario's with her warm, inviting smile hinting at far more.

Jeff shook his head and said, "Thanks, but I think that's it for me today. Have a nice one."

She shrugged, disappointed, but took his empty cup and walked away.

Maybe there was another way. He left the shop and crossed Claire Avenue, where the parlor was, and walked along the cross street to the alleyway running between the rows of houses and garages. As he looked up the alley, he caught a glimpse of her turning at the far end of the block—no one else had such flaming red hair. He started running. This must have been why he never saw her come or go from the house: she used the back door.

Halfway up the alley, he realized this was a stupid idea. He needed something subtle. What he needed was for her to come to him.

Checking to be sure he was past the parlor, Jeff walked between two garages that opened onto the alley and found a place out of sight. *She has to come back, right?*

Someone had put a half-height brick wall behind their trash cans to demarcate the end of their lot, or maybe to keep a small dog inside, though he saw no evidence of one. Some loose papers had missed the cans and lay on the ground next to them, and one of the lids was sitting loose on top. Brushing some of the dust and dirt off the wall, he hopped up, sat facing the alleyway, and waited. *At least you won't be chasing after her down the street.*

About twenty long minutes later he heard footsteps, but it turned out to be three young boys who gave him a funny look and crossed the alley to avoid him. After another ten minutes or so, he heard another set of footsteps approaching, but they stopped.

After a moment, he heard her voice. "Where are you? Jeff, I know you're here."

Slowly, trying not to spook her, he hopped off the wall and inched out to the edge of the pavement. His view was partially blocked by one of the garages, but the sun behind her lit up her hair like a torch. He stared at her for a moment. "How did you know I was here?"

"Come out where I can see you."

He did, walking to about fifteen feet from her, paranoid about getting closer lest she run.

Her expression was wary, but curious. "What do you want from me?"

Putting his arms behind him, he said, "Please, I need to talk to you. I need to talk to someone who won't think I'm crazy."

"Why would they?"

The breeze flipped off the lid off a trash can and it fell into the alley, landing on edge. It rolled about twenty feet with the wind behind it, starting to fall before righting itself and rolling upwind to clatter onto the ground next to the can it was originally on.

Realizing what she saw, Anya's eyes went wide and she seemed at a loss for words. She looked down at the ground, then at Jeff. "I see. Why me?"

"After Friday, I kind of hoped you could help me, or at least listen to me and tell me I'm not crazy."

After a moment, she pursed her lips, thinking. "No. You are crazy."

It took a moment before her words clicked. He chuckled. "Hmm, well I guess that settles that."

A small grin crept over her face. "Is there anything else you want from me?"

Jeff looked back to the ground and it was a long time before he looked up and searched her face. "Everything."

Anya's eyes popped open wide and her lips parted, forming a small O. She took a step backwards. Only momentarily startled, she regained her composure and her mouth settled into a grin that reflected in her eyes. She watched him for a moment. "Well, at least you're telling the truth this time."

CHAPTER 5

The following morning, they met at the coffee shop. Jeff had called in sick to work ... this was far more important. Anya wouldn't start doing readings until later today, so she had some free time.

"My mother told me not to see you. I don't know how she figured out we met, but she seemed sure we had. And she still doesn't want you anywhere near the house, or me."

"Wait. Your mother?"

She nodded. "AKA Madam Onofre."

"What, she hates me for no reason?"

Anya shook her head. "No, she said something about my father, but she wouldn't give me details. She never wants to talk about him when I bring it up. I'm guessing something bad happened, but I'm not sure."

"Where is he?"

"For some reason, I think he's dead. I haven't seen him since I was about four years old. I barely remember him."

21

Looking across the table at her, he took a sip of his coffee as she did the same. "You know, I know nothing about you other than you are incredibly beautiful and have the most amazing hair. The first time I saw you it seemed like your hair was moving all by itself."

She grinned. "Yeah, sometimes it seems that way. So, what do you want to know?"

"Like I said—everything."

"Well, when you said that yesterday you meant a lot more than knowing about me."

He shrugged. "True, but it's a start."

She thought for a few moments. "But I'm boring!"

"Somehow, I can't imagine that for a second. You never told me how you knew I was there when you came down the alley."

She frowned, narrowing her eyes. "It's hard to explain. I know when you're close. When you came to see my mom the other day, I was upstairs in my bedroom. I knew you were there the minute you walked into the house and wasn't sure what to do. Ever since Friday when we met, you're there in my mind, all the time."

"Same for me. I woke up with a hangover on Saturday and the first thing I thought about was you … couldn't get you out of my thoughts. I've been ignoring phone calls from my friends, my mother. I wanted to find you, meet you, et cetera."

She laughed. "Yeah, it's the et cetera part that worries me."

Surprised, he said, "Does it really?"

She looked down, face turning a light pink, and shook her head. "Yes and no. On the one hand I want to go back to the way things were a few days ago, but another part of me wants to know a lot more about you and why you're here, and why I keep thinking about you. It's exciting, in a good way. But you wanted to talk, so talk."

Jeff looked around the shop. There were few customers in there and most of those were coming in for a cup of coffee to go and turning around to leave. He figured it was safe enough. The only way he could see them getting more privacy was going back to his apartment, but he wasn't about to suggest that.

"This all started a couple of years ago, right after I got out of college. One day I was sitting at my desk with my feet up and dropped a pencil on the floor. I thought it would be nice if I didn't have to lean down and get it, so I pictured it floating up and on to the desk. It did, but by the time it got halfway there I was so startled I fell out of my chair.

"It seemed totally random, but then I tried it again. Took me about an hour to do it the second time, but I got the pencil up on the desk, placed where I wanted it. It was incredibly cool, but it worried me, too. This stuff only happens in fantasies, right?

"After figuring it out. I practiced a little every day and it got easier. Now it's almost second nature, but I can't say it's good for much. And it scares me. I thought about talking to my friends or my mom about it, but figured they would think I was nuts. So, I kept it to myself till now."

They had avoided any physical contact, but Anya, not even thinking, reached across the table to put her hand over his. The shock was still there, but not so strong. She started and raised her hand, but when she realized it wasn't as bad, she lowered her hand back, wrapping her fingers into Jeff's. It felt like a tiny electrical current pulsed back and forth between them, warming and not at all unpleasant.

"Well, this is better," she commented.

Jeff nodded. "Yeah, I kind of like it. I could get used to this." He gave her a smile and squeezed her fingers.

"Me, too," she murmured. After a pause while they sat there holding hands, she added, "And I don't think you're crazy."

"Maybe I am," he said. "About you."

CHAPTER 6

"I told you to stay away from him. What on earth do you think you're doing?"

Anya frowned, stomping her foot, anger building. "I'm an adult, Mom, in case you hadn't noticed. I can do what I want and see who I want."

Beatriz, standing by the sink, glared at her. "You have no idea what you are getting into. I'm trying to protect you."

"From what exactly?"

"This guy will bring you trouble and heartache. Leave him alone and you'll thank me for it later."

Anya put her hands on her hips. "No!" She glared at her mother for what seemed like an hour. "What do you have against him? He's nice to me, he likes me, all we do is talk."

"For now."

"So what? I never get to have a boyfriend? I stay here with you doing readings for the rest of my life? I never get out and find my own way and do what I want?"

"Don't be stupid. He's the wrong one for you. You'll find someone else."

"I don't get it. What do you have against him?"

"I know his kind."

"What kind is that? He's a guy. He wants the same things all guys want. It's normal. And I'm not stupid. I know the kinds of things he will want, but I get to decide what happens here, not you."

"There are things going on here you don't understand."

Getting further annoyed by these cryptic statements, Anya said, "Like what? Maybe you should tell me. And how do you know, anyway? Don't tell me it's because you're psychic, either, I'm not buying that one again."

Beatriz sighed. "I know what happened to me and I don't want the same thing for you."

Anya frowned. Her mother had never mentioned anything like this before, and she wasn't sure where this conversation was going. "Maybe you should tell me what happened."

"It's complicated." Beatriz wrung her hands for a moment and glared at her daughter. "I don't want to talk about it."

"Is this about Dad?"

PLEASE, SISTER

"Anya, it's too painful for me to talk about it."

Not to be put off, the girl replied, "You never told me what happened to him. He disappeared one day and never came back. Do you even know? Where did he go?"

"Anya…" She pulled a chair out from the kitchen table and sat down, burying her face in her hands. "I didn't tell you because I have no way of knowing, but I think I know."

Her daughter got a glass of water and set it on the table in front of her, then pulled up a chair and waited.

"We were both young when we met, younger than you. I was doing readings with your grandmother and met this really nice, handsome guy. But he had some secrets I didn't know about until later.

"We fell in love quickly and it was so wonderful. We were both very happy and then you came along and it was even better. It was only later when I learned what he could do … he did things, merely by thinking about them. It scared me at first, but I got used to the idea and after a while it didn't bother me much anymore.

"Whenever we touched, it was magic. He made me tingle, and said it was the same for him. God, we were happy.

"One day he got into trouble with a bad bunch of people. He'd been gambling and owed them money, more than we had. I was scared and so was he, but he found a way out. He started helping them out with some of their activities. At first it was nothing serious, stuff like breaking windows to warn people who were behind in their payments. But he got more involved. Breaking and entering, stealing stuff. I worried about him all the time, but he said he had it under control.

"When you were four, he was out helping them one night. I never found out all the details but he had talked earlier in the afternoon about going to the police for help getting out of his mess. Well, they did another break-in that night and the cops showed up. There was shooting, but he got away and some of the gang got caught. He phoned and told me he needed to go away for a while, but he'd be back. That was in December so he went to Florida, figuring he would be safe.

"About two weeks later I was lying in bed one night and it felt like my heart was being torn out of my body … worse than a heart attack, worse than childbirth. It was more painful than I thought I could endure. And the little spark of him that was always with me disappeared. I knew he was dead, but I didn't know where or how or who killed him. He was gone. To this day, I have never been able to find out anything."

Anya's eyes went wide, astounded. "I remember that night. You started screaming and I didn't know what to do. I came in to help you, but you were lost in your pain, I guess. You wouldn't even talk to me."

CHAPTER 7

Jeff got home from work on Wednesday and opened his apartment door to find his sister sitting on the couch, finishing a margarita. "Did you fix one for me, too?"

"I can if you want. Come to think of it, maybe it's a good idea." She got up and went into the kitchen while Jeff dropped some papers on his desk, wondering where this conversation was headed.

Laura came back in with two drinks and handed one to him. "Why don't you sit down?"

"Is this about you and Marcus?"

She shook her head. "Nope." With a smile, she added, "I want to know what's going on with you since you're not talking to anyone all of a sudden."

Jeff took a sip of his drink. "Hmm, needs salt." He headed for the kitchen.

Over his shoulder, he heard Laura say, "I can stay here as long as it takes."

Shaking his head, he walked back into the living room and handed her the salt shaker and sat down. "What do you want to know?"

"Let's start with why you aren't answering your phone or calling people back the last few days."

Hedging, he said, "Well, I've been pretty busy with work the last few days, you know?"

"Like Saturday, and Sunday? Oh, and you weren't at work on Monday either, were you? And you won't even call Mom back." She let her question hang in the air, waiting for him.

"Look, I'm okay now. I'll call people back. We can all go out Friday night, like usual."

She pursed her lips. "You're lying. I can always tell. You never learned how to hide it, at least not from me."

"Can you drop it? It's not your problem."

"Oh, you have a problem! We're making progress. Does this have anything to do with getting thrown out of the palm readers' place on Friday?"

He took a big drink from his glass, considering what to say.

Laura smiled, tilting her head to the side. "You rarely gulp your drinks. Did I hit on a nerve here? What did happen that night? You never told us and haven't talked to us since."

He shook his head. "Do we really have to go over this

now?"

She smiled again. It was starting to annoy him. "Two options, bro, you either tell me now, or I call Mom and you can tell us both when she gets here."

Giving in, he said, "Fine. Almost nothing happened. I got thrown out almost as soon as I got there."

"Yes, but why? Did you try to hurt her?"

"Don't be ridiculous."

"Did you ask her out? She was gorgeous, I'll give you that. Wish I looked that good. But you've never fallen for a pretty face before, you've always wanted more, and you've never been in a hurry to start something."

"No. I sat down at the table. She wasn't in the room at the time. When she walked in, well, yes, I thought she was beautiful and I told her so, but it didn't seem to bother her. So, she sat down and I put out my hand. When she touched me, there was an electric spark between us, like static electricity only much stronger. I jumped up and knocked over my chair, and she jumped up and backed against the wall, scared to death. Then she threw us out of her house. That was it, that was all that happened."

"So this is all about Sister Anna?"

"Anya."

"I'll take that as a confession. Have you seen her

since then?"

"The following day I got thrown out of her house by her mother, Madam Onofre. Then I kind of ran into Anya on Sunday."

"Wait, you were stalking her?"

He shifted his eyes back and forth. "Kind of. I only wanted to talk to her again. I wouldn't hurt her … just talk."

"So, I take it you did talk to her?"

"We spoke for a few minutes on Sunday and met for coffee Monday morning at the coffee shop on the corner."

"You skipped out on work to meet a girl at a coffee shop? You've never done anything like that before. And you're acting like somebody else. What did you do with my brother?"

He ignored her.

"Are you seeing her again?" Laura pressed.

"She's not doing readings tomorrow, so we're meeting for dinner."

"I'm confused here. Why would you go out with somebody when you'll get shocked every time you touch them?"

"In the coffee shop, she accidentally put her hand on

mine. There was a little shock, but not like the first one. It felt warm and tingly."

Laura's eyes widened. "God, you've got it bad, don't you? Why was she putting her hand on yours ... is she interested?"

"Look, drop it and leave me alone." Angry, and without even thinking, he picked up her keys from the table by the door and threw them onto the couch next to her. Without getting up.

The smug look on Laura's face was replaced by panic. "Holy shit. What the hell happened?"

"Oh, crap." He shook his head. How had he been so stupid?

"Jeff, you're scaring me. How did my keys get across the room?"

Rather than answer, he lifted her two inches off the couch and dropped her.

Laura bounced up, then leapt to her feet. "What? How? Are you doing that?"

Jeff hung his head and shook it, and spoke quietly. "Sit down, please. We need to talk."

Laura was still wild-eyed, but the calm and defeat in his voice gave her enough confidence to sit back down, though she never took her eyes from him.

"It's why I needed to talk to her. I need someone who

won't think I'm either crazy or a freak."

"But we … when did you start doing this?"

"About two years ago, but please, you can't tell anyone. I was scared at first, but decided to keep it quiet. I don't want people thinking I'm a weirdo."

It took about a minute for Laura to process all the information and realize what he was going through. Cocking her head to the side, she asked, "So is she the one you need for this?"

"When I waited for her in the alley, I was out of sight. She stopped before she could see me because she knew I was there. She could feel me."

Laura looked skeptical. "She felt you?"

"I don't know how, like I don't know how I do what I do. She can't explain it either."

"Jeff…"

"Laura, promise me you won't say anything to anyone. Please?"

"Not even Mom?"

"God, especially not her. This has to be our secret or I won't be able to live a normal life."

She stared at him and slowly shook her head. "What do you mean by normal…?" She paused. "Oh, shit." After another pause, she shook her head. "Hate to say this, but it sounds like you two were made for each other. And, yeah, I'll keep it quiet as long as you don't use it on me again."

That brought a wry chuckle. "You got a deal."

CHAPTER 8

Anya was waiting at the coffee shop when Jeff drove up. "Oh, you have a car, too. Nice!"

"It shows how little we know about each other. Are you sure you want to get in a car with a stranger?"

"As long as you don't offer me candy, I'll feel safe."

Jeff pretended to search the car. "Hmm, don't see any. Hop in."

She grinned at him as they drove off, heading to an Italian restaurant a couple of miles away. When they pulled up, he asked, "Is this okay? It's usually pretty quiet and the food is good if you like Italian."

She nodded. "Sure, I've never been here before, but I trust your judgment."

At Jeff's request, the hostess seated them at a table in a quiet corner and handed them menus. "Your server will be Kathleen. She'll be here in a minute."

"A server with an Irish name in an Italian restaurant. I guess we're going multi-ethnic tonight," commented Anya.

PLEASE, SISTER

Kathleen came over with two glasses of water and asked for drink orders.

Jeff stumbled with this. Looking at Anya, he said, "Do you mind if I have some wine?"

That was met with a laugh. "Of course you can." Smiling at the waitress she added, "I'll have water."

As the waitress walked away, Jeff turned back to Anya. "I feel so stupid. I don't even know how old you are."

"I turn twenty next month on the 23rd. Be sure you remember."

"So, what else should I know about you?"

"I told you before, I'm boring. Mostly Mom and I hang around the house doing readings. I graduated from high school about two years ago and didn't want to go to college at first, but it seems I'm in a rut already. We do readings, go to the grocery store, and cook. Boring stuff."

Jeff shrugged. "Doesn't sound so bad. I guess you meet a lot of people."

"Well, yes and no. Lots of them come in for readings, but it's not like I sit down and have conversations with them. It's pretty one-sided. And I don't go out much. Once in a while we'll drive over to the mall for shopping, but not very often. The rest of the time I mostly read."

"What do you like to read?"

"Oh, you know. French philosophers, physics journals, plus I go through the entire encyclopedia every month. And I have to read the current *Today's Psychic* to stay up to date on what's happening in the industry." She grinned at him.

"What, no steamy romances?"

"Oh, those too. I read them to put me to sleep at night."

"Oddly, they seem to have a different effect on me."

"You read romances?" she asked skeptically.

"Rarely, but I need to stay up to date on the latest techniques, you know?"

They both laughed as the waitress brought Jeff's drink, followed in a couple of minutes by the food.

"This really smells good," she said, inhaling the fragrance from her lasagna, "but I have a question."

"Okay, Anya, what?"

"Can I try a sip of your red wine?"

"Is anybody looking right now?"

"No."

He handed her his glass and she took a small sip, then quickly handed it back to him. Pausing to savor it, she added, "Wow! Good stuff. You know, I'll be glad when I can drink legally. I have a glass of white wine at home once in a while, but only rarely."

As they started eating, the hostess seated a large party next to them and it got noisy. Jeff frowned, but there was nothing he could do. Rather than try to talk, they focused on their food.

As they finished up and Jeff paid the bill, Anya said, "Could we go back to your place for a while?" Seeing the surprised look he gave her, she added, "No, not for that. To talk."

He snapped his fingers in mock disappointment. "Sure," then added, "I know it will be quiet there."

Anya was quiet on the short drive, but she seemed to perk up once they got to his apartment building. "This seems like a nice place. How long have you lived here?"

"Since shortly after I got out of college. I found a job pretty quickly and leased it once I started. So, about two years."

"You got out of college? Were they holding you prisoner?"

"On occasion it seemed like it." He unlocked the door and let her in, flipped on the lights and set his keys on the table.

Anya put her purse on the couch, taking her time,

looking around the room, taking everything in: the chair, posters on the wall, the blanket over the couch, even the faint floral scent. "This is nice, Jeff." She turned back to him and paused for a moment. "Kiss me."

He put his hands around her waist and pulled her closer, touching his lips to hers. The warm electric feeling was tantalizing. He pulled back and looked into her eyes, then pulled her tight against him and kissed her again, parting his lips as she did the same. When they separated, Anya said, "Wow. That was really nice."

Jeff slowly released her and said, "I need to use the bathroom. I'll be right back. Make yourself at home." As he walked away, she peeked into the kitchen and bedroom.

When he was washing his hands, he heard women's voices. One was definitely Anya's, but the other was too quiet to identify, so he went back to the living room.

Anya was chatting with Laura, and Jeff shook his head. "So much for talking."

"Oh Jeff, stop it," his sister said. "Mom asked me to drop off this book you loaned her and I didn't think you'd be here. By the way, she didn't like it."

Anya picked up the book and looked at him. "You read Sartre?"

"I read lots of things. His philosophy is interesting but his politics are terrible."

Laura said, "This is great. It gives me a chance to have some girl talk with Anya. Maybe you should run out and get us some pizza."

"We just ate."

Laura put on a hurt expression. "But you don't want me to starve, do you?"

"Maybe so. And I think I should take your key away, too."

Laura grinned. "Maybe I should give it to Anya!"

Anya laughed as Jeff pretended to get angry.

"What's the matter? Were you hoping for some private time with your girlfriend?"

Jeff shook his head in resignation. "What do you want on the pizza?"

CHAPTER 9

After Laura finally left, Jeff and Anya did get some time alone.

"Laura seems nice and friendly. That was the same impression I got when I did her reading."

Jeff had gotten distracted staring at her, so he shook his head, coming back to the present. "Yeah, mostly she is, though she likes to butt into other people's business once in a while."

Anya smiled, "Oh, it's normal girl stuff. She wants to make sure you're happy."

"Are you like that, too?"

"Yes, but I don't have any siblings to use it on. I want to see you happy, and I know what you're thinking … forget it. At least for now."

"She seemed happy after her reading. Did you tell her she was going to marry Marcus? We speculated about it."

"Sorry, can't answer. Readings are confidential." She got a quizzical look. "So, do I get to meet the rest of your family, too?"

"Sure, soon, I guess. What about your mom?"

"Oh, I've already met her."

He frowned at her, lips pressed together, keeping silent.

She grinned again. "Oh, you mean you? Hmm, that's a more difficult issue. Though you did meet her."

"Yeah. It didn't go very well, did it?"

"No, but if I bring you over, she'll have to be nice to you."

"Are you sure?"

"Pretty much." She paused, looking around the room. "Jeff, could I stay here tonight?"

His eyebrows shot up and eyes widened. "Really?"

"No sex, I want to cuddle with you."

"Ah, I see. You want to torture me. Did you bring pajamas?" He looked at her with a very I'm-interested-in-you expression.

"I thought maybe you could loan me something."

"Settle for shorts or a big tee-shirt?"

She pressed her lips together. "If you make this too difficult, I'll go home."

"Okay, okay. Yes, I have some stuff you can wear

though they'll be big on you."

"And you have to promise to behave."

"What exactly do you mean?"

"You can kiss me, but that's about all. No hands under the clothes stuff."

"Well, I guess I can do that…"

Smiling shyly, she added, "We'll get to the rest later, but not tonight."

Jeff grinned. "I like the sound of that. Should you call your mother to let her know?"

"Probably should, but I'm not going to. Can we watch some television for a while?"

"Sure. You want some wine?"

"Yep, but remember, it won't loosen my morals."

After a glass of wine and an hour of TV, they both yawned, so they turned off the show and went into the bedroom. Jeff got out some clothes for her and gave her a new toothbrush and in a few minutes she came out of the bathroom with the oversize top hanging loose over the shorts.

"It's all I can do to keep from drooling," he commented.

"Gross!"

He headed into the bathroom then stuck his head out. "Do you want me to wear a tee-shirt or just my shorts."

"A pair of shorts is okay, I guess."

"You sure you won't lose control when you see my sexy abs?"

"Jeff, I can still change my mind…"

"I can take a hint."

A few minutes later he came out and found her sitting in bed reading the Sartre book, but when he crawled in next to her, she set it down and turned off the light, settling in with her back to him.

He pulled her gently over onto her back and gave her a long kiss. As she settled back onto her side again, he slipped his hand over her shirt, cradling her breast.

"Hey, you're cheating."

"I'm not under your clothes."

"Hmm, you're right," she responded. "Well, it does feel nice."

They cuddled close, and, eventually, fell asleep.

CHAPTER 10

"Are you sure this is a good idea?"

Anya looked over at him. "Are you scared?"

"Not exactly, but meeting your mother again after you've spent the night at my apartment … it doesn't seem like optimum timing," Jeff replied.

"Hmm, optimum timing. I'll have to remember that. Don't worry about it. Since I'm bringing you, there's not much she can do about it."

"Does she have a gun?"

"Well, yes. In this neighborhood it's a good idea, but she won't shoot you."

As they walked up the alley nearing her house, a young man stepped out in front of them, brandishing a knife. He was average height, very thin, probably in his late teens, and he looked angry. "Give me your money, all of it, and you don't get hurt."

Jeff pretended to reach for his wallet and, using his mind, slammed the kid in the chest without moving a muscle. The boy fell backwards and slid about five feet, his knife skittering away. Keeping his eyes on the two of them, he jumped to his feet and ran off, forgetting about his knife.

Anya shook her head. "It might have been better to give him our money. I'm not sure."

"At least this talent I have is good for something."

"Perhaps. Let's go meet Mom."

It was still early, since readings started about three o'clock, so Beatriz was still in the kitchen, wearing a slightly worn house dress and slippers. She looked up from her tea as they walked in. She waited, watching.

Anya said, "Mom, I want you to get to know Jeff better. I really like him and I want you two to get along. Do you think you can do that?"

"You're talking to your mother. Show some respect."

Anya glared at her. "I will if you will."

"He has a bad influence on you already, the way you talk."

"You're underestimating me, Mom."

"Where were you last night … with him?"

Anya nodded. "Yes, though it's probably not what you think."

"Maybe, for now." Looking over at Jeff, she said, "Sit

down. Maybe Anya will make some tea for all of us."

Jeff sat, unsure what approach, if any, might work; he opted for truth. "She's right, ma'am, it's not what it looks like."

Beatriz shook her head, still frowning. "I know how these things go. I was young once, if you can believe that."

"Umm … yeah, of course. I wanted to meet you and hoped we could come to some kind of a truce."

"Are we at war?"

"Kind of feels like it to me."

She gave him a small smile. "You know, you remind me of someone I knew long ago."

Anya set the tea on the table and pulled up a chair next to Jeff.

"See," she continued, "she even sits next to you, across from me. You're both against me."

Jeff shook his head. "All I want is to make Anya happy."

Beatriz laughed cynically. "Can you? How much do you even know about her—or her about you?"

Unwilling to get sucked into an argument, Jeff said, "We're learning. It's all we're doing at this stage, part of a normal process."

"So she spends the night with you?"

Anya changed the subject, "Who does he remind you of, that you're so worried about it."

Beatriz frowned at her daughter. "Your father … and me."

Anya caught her breath, but recovered and said, "But you two were happy for a long time."

Beatriz nodded. "Until we weren't. It's what I worry about for you … the part when you aren't."

"But, Mom, that's part of life. Sometimes it's good, and sometimes not. Everyone goes through it."

"Enough of this, I won't talk about us anymore. We'll talk about you."

Anya frowned. "Okay, what do you want to know?"

Looking at Jeff, Beatriz asked, "Do you have a job, family?"

He nodded. "Both. I've been working for the last two years, since I graduated from college. I have a Mom and sister. My Dad died right before my graduation."

"Are you rich?"

Anya jumped in, "Mom, what kind of question is that?"

Ignoring her, Beatriz asked Jeff, "What will you do when you get her pregnant?"

"Mom!"

Jeff waved Anya off and turned to her mom. After a moment of thought, he said, "Actually, I can't think of anything I would like more."

Anya turned to him and stared, eyes wide. Her mouth widened into a huge grin. "Really?"

He kissed her, not rushing, and said, "Yes, absolutely."

Beatriz rolled her eyes. "I was afraid of that." She stared at Jeff for a moment, observing him, then stuck out her hand. "Fine. Truce. But be good to her or I'll curse you."

Anya burst out laughing. "Did you learn how to do curses last night while I was gone?"

CHAPTER 11

"What have you been doing the last two weeks, and why was it so important that I come over tonight?" Laura asked.

"I need your help," Jeff responded.

Anya walked in the door, carrying a handful of clothing and dresses.

Laura gawked. "You're moving in already?"

Jeff said, "Yes. That's why I need your help. To bring in her stuff and to give her your key so I don't have to pay for another one."

Anya came back out of the bedroom, having put her clothing on the bed until they could figure out how to arrange everything. Laura ran over to her and gave her a big hug.

Startled, Anya backed up, eyes wide, bumping into the wall. "What was that for?"

"Welcome to the family!" she responded.

"Oh, umm, thanks."

Laura turned to her brother and said, "Jeff, I'm amazed at you. You're settling down. I thought it would never happen."

"Laura, I'm twenty-three and I can figure out what I want to do. And that is to spend the rest of my life with Anya, no matter what you or anyone else thinks."

"Oh, Jeff, I'm so happy for you."

He frowned at her. "Could you help carry some clothes?"

"Of course. It's a party. I'm calling Marcus too."

"Laura, there's not that much to carry…"

"I'll even buy the pizza. Come on, let's do this." Turning to Anya, she said, "What kind do you like?"

"Well, I guess pepperoni."

"Anchovies?"

"Good grief, no."

"Avocados?"

"Do they put them on pizza?"

"No, it was a test. Okay, no avocados. Anything else?"

Jeff stepped in front of his sister. "Are you delirious?"

She hugged him. "No. Happy for you. I've been

waiting for this a long time."

Jeff smirked, "So now it's your turn, huh?"

"AAACH! Don't go there right now. One of us at a time."

Looking over at Anya, he said "Well, I guess it only works one way."

Anya chuckled while Laura frowned at him. His sister picked up the phone and ordered pizza, then called Marcus and told him to get over here, quick.

As Laura ran out the door to get a load of clothes, Jeff put his hand over his face for a moment, but dropped it and turned to Anya. "I'm sorry, this is getting out of hand."

She grinned and came over to give him a long kiss. "It's alright … fine, actually. Speaking of getting out of hand…" She took his right hand and placed it over her breast, holding it tight.

He laughed. "I could get used to this."

"I certainly hope so."

A couple of hours later, all of Anya's clothes were put away, though perhaps not in their final place. The pizza and beer, contributions from Marcus, were gone and Jeff and Anya were left alone.

"Tired?" he asked.

"A little, but not too much. However, bed is sounding more attractive by the moment."

"I'll lock the front door and clean up this mess while you get ready."

She came out of the bathroom in a pair of boy shorts and tank top. After Jeff took a moment to admire her, he grabbed his sleep shorts and went to brush his teeth and change.

He expected that she would be reading when he returned, but she wasn't. She sat slouching against the pillow with the sheet tucked under her arms, revealing bare shoulders. He glanced around the room and saw both pieces of her night clothes thrown across a nearby chair. He smiled at her. "Are you, by any chance, trying to seduce me?"

"Aren't you my lover?"

"Oh, definitely."

He sat on the edge of the bed and slipped off his shorts, and pulled the sheet up over him as he slid under the covers.

She grinned at him, looking a little nervous.

"We don't have to do this, you know. We could wait."

Quietly, she said, "Shut up and kiss me."

So, he did. It started with a brief kiss. He took longer as she opened her mouth to him and her tongue met his, playing.

He put his hand on the side of her head, holding her face in front of his. "I would do anything for you."

"Do you love me?"

"More than life itself."

Still quiet, she said, "Me too."

As he pulled her closer to him, the sheet slipped down, revealing a bare breast. He gently put his hand on it, rubbing his thumb across her nipple. She let out a gentle sigh in response.

After a few moments of that, he grabbed the top edge of the sheet and pulled it back, throwing it off the foot of the bed. Anya made no motion to cover herself; she looked at him with watery eyes.

"Are you going to cry?"

"Maybe ... I'm not sure. I'm so happy."

He pulled her naked body down so she was flat on the bed, on her back, and rolled on top of her slowly. He started kissing her again.

First was her forehead, which got a couple of small pecks before he moved down to her eyelids. As she sighed again, relaxing into the feeling, he moved to her earlobe and spent some kisses on that, sucking gently, before she grabbed his head in her hands and put his mouth on hers.

She was not shy, though she was tentative, and he noticed that. "Scared?"

Anya shook her head. "That's not the right word … I'm not sure."

"Happy?"

"Mmm, yes."

He kissed her lips for a while, getting more and more passionate. He stopped. She looked up into his eyes, wondering.

Slowly, he took each of her arms and extended them fully, hands out to about the level of her head, his hands in hers. Very gently, he slid his feet between hers and pushed her legs apart.

Anya started laughing.

Jeff looked into her face, kissed her neck as she tilted her head back to let him. "What are you laughing at?"

She chuckled again. "Is this the da Vinci position?"

He laughed too. "Could be. Maybe we should call it that." Taking his time, he slid down on the bed and placed his lips on her breasts, one at a time, taking special care to suck on each nipple until they were both fully erect.

Again, he slid himself down the bed, kissing her stomach and sending his tongue into her navel. Her breath was getting shorter.

One more time he slid down, nibbling gently on each of her hip bones before burying his face between her thighs, starting to lick slowly. She raised both her legs and leaned them out to the sides so he had complete access to her.

At first, he used his tongue to probe her and Anya caught her breath a few times. Slowly, he found what he was searching for and sucked it gently into his mouth. Slowly, again, and again. Her breath got shorter and shorter as he kept sucking.

He glanced up at her ... eyes closed, head tilted back. The first spasm surprised him, but he kept sucking, gently, until she was satisfied.

"Oh, Jeff..."

As her body started to calm, he rested his head there, his mouth still on her, catching his breath. It was about a minute or so when he felt her about to move. So he started again, slowly sucking on her.

She looked down. "What?"

He said nothing, but continued coaxing her, wanting nothing more than her enjoyment.

In a few seconds, she stopped objecting, but let herself drift into the feeling. Looking up, he saw the smile on her face as she closed her eyes once again to lose herself. It wasn't long before her second orgasm swept over her. She arched her back as it went on and on.

As her body cooled down, she looked at him. "I'm so embarrassed. That was so quick."

Lifting his head, he shook it. "Don't be. Enjoy it. That's what I'm here for." With that, he pulled himself up the bed and slid into her.

She gasped at first, but wrapped her legs around him and pulled him further in, as he kissed her lips, her mouth, everything.

Trying to sense her body, he bit his tongue to slow himself down, but it didn't help much. As he felt her contracting around him, he let himself go, matching her spasms with his own.

When they were finished, Jeff laid there, still deep inside her. *God, I want to stay here forever.*

As he faded, he slipped out of her. Still kissing her lips, he noticed that she was relaxing totally, letting him do anything he wanted.

He rolled off of her, still holding on to her and caressing her breasts with his lips, his hands. As he rolled back to face her, she turned with him.

"That was amazing."

He nodded. "Yes, you are."

She pulled up the sheet over them both and put her head on his chest. "Sleep well."

***

In the morning, Anya was the first to wake up. She shifted around to face him and nibbled on his chest, then noticed the tent near his waist. Moving slowly so she wouldn't wake him, she slid the covers off and looked at him, erect as he still slept.

She slid down the bed, trying not to wake him. Keeping her eyes on his face, she lowered her lips onto him.

At first, he moaned, still asleep. His eyes flew open and he looked down to see her gently sucking on him. The brief fear that woke him disappeared as he lay back, watching Anya's eyes move up and down, lost in the feeling, still amazed by her radiant hair. Finally, he could take it no more and threw his head back, giving in to the feeling.

A few minutes later, he pulled her into his arms and kissed her face, her mouth, her ears. "That's a hell of a way to wake up," he grinned. "And what do you want this morning?"

She laughed at him. "I think three orgasms in one night are enough for me. How about breakfast?"

CHAPTER 12

Several days later, Anya had finished dressing when there was a knock on the door. Jeff had gone into work early that morning for an important meeting, and he would have used his key anyway. Looking through the peephole, she saw a middle-aged woman she didn't recognize. She put the chain on the door before she opened it a crack. "May I help you?"

The woman smiled warmly. "So you're the lovely Anya that Laura has been talking about so much. I'm Jeff's mom, Lainie. Thought I'd stop by before work and see if you were free for breakfast."

Anya took the chain off the door and invited her in.

Lainie stood back to get a good look at her for a moment, then she said, "Wow! You are pretty. Laura was right."

Embarrassed, Anya said, "Thanks."

"Oh, I guess I shouldn't have said that, even if it is true. Can I give you a hug?"

Anya nodded and Lainie threw her arms around her. "It is really a pleasure to meet you. I know Jeff would have brought you over soon, but all I've heard from Laura lately was 'Anya, Anya, Anya.' I hope you don't mind me dropping in on you like this." Looking around, she asked "Is Jeff still here?"

"No, he went into work early. I was going to go over to my mother's house but there's no hurry. Breakfast would be great."

"Perfect. I don't have to be at work till ten, so we can talk over food and then I can drop you off wherever."

"Sounds good to me, let me get my jacket."

The diner they went to was only a few blocks away, so they didn't get a chance to talk much on the way. When they got there, the smells of bacon and coffee, especially, greeted them. Both of them ordered the house special, a three-egg omelet with everything, and coffee.

"So, Laura said you met because they went to have their fortunes told?"

"Well, actually I read palms, though there is a little bit of fortune telling involved, too."

"How on earth did you get involved with that?"

"Oh, my mom has been doing it for years, and my grandmother before her. I guess it runs in the family."

Lainie paused for a moment. "Would you read mine?"

Anya pretended to be shocked—"Without my robe

and scarf? And no candles!" They both laughed as Anya took Lainie's hand, examining the lines on her palm. After about a minute, Anya frowned briefly, and then smiled again as she looked up. "Well, things are certainly looking up for you. It seems like your new job is going to work out well. Jeff told me about the job, but it looks like you'll stay there for a long time. From what I see here, it also looks like Laura may be moving out in the near future. And then, the interesting part … a new romance is coming soon."

"Wait, I'm not even looking for anything like that. Haven't been since my husband went and died on me. I can't imagine going through that again."

Anya nodded. "Sometimes things have a way of sneaking up on you."

"Like you and Jeff?"

Anya nodded, still looking at Lainie's palm. "Exactly like that. It sure caught me by surprise and at first, I thought I never wanted to see him again, but I couldn't get him out of my mind. Oh! Now I see why, this guy drives a Corvette."

"Please tell me it's not a little red one."

Anya shook her head and grinned. "Nope, definitely not red."

They were about to continue but the waitress brought their breakfasts, so Anya dropped Lainie's hand and they concentrated on eating, chatting between bites.

CHAPTER 13

Anya was working that night, so it was about nine when Jeff came by to pick her up. "How was today, sweetheart?"

"I like it when you call me that. It was fun, especially this morning when your mom came by the apartment."

"What? Let me guess, Laura was talking about you so she 'happened' to drop by."

"Not exactly, she came by to take me out to breakfast."

"Well, I guess that works. Sometimes I wish my family could wait for me to do things, though. So how was breakfast?"

"It was good. Your mom is nice and friendly and very talkative."

"She's in sales, of course she is." Glancing over at her, he said, "You seem distracted. Is something wrong?"

"Jeff, when we get home, I want to talk to you about something."

"Not in the car?"

"No. I want your full attention."

"Oh-oh, this sounds ominous."

"Drive."

When they got to the apartment, Jeff tossed his papers down and poured a glass of wine for each of them. They settled on the couch. "Okay, I'm all yours."

Anya rubbed her arms and frowned, unsure how to approach this. "Well, really, I shouldn't be talking to you about this, but I feel like I need to."

Jeff sipped his wine, waiting.

"When your mom and I were at the diner we were talking about palm reading and she asked me if I would do hers, so I did. Most of it was fine and I told her that part, but one thing I noticed was something worrying, so I didn't say anything to her. It's the kind of thing I've only seen once before.

"There is something bad that is going to happen in her life. Not right away, but not ten years from now, either. I couldn't tell what it was, but when I looked at one particular line on her palm, all I saw was blackness in the future. That is not a good sign at all. I even talked to my mom about it. She says she has seen that on occasion, but not often. The only feedback she ever heard was from one of her regulars who had this but stopped showing up every week. Two months later she came back and said she had been in the hospital.

"Now this doesn't mean your mom is going to the hospital or anything like that. On the other hand, it does seem alarming. That's why I didn't mention it to her ... I didn't know enough to help and I wasn't going to worry her when I could be wrong and nothing may ever happen."

Jeff shook his head, thinking, looking down for a moment. "I see why you didn't want to talk with her about this, for a couple of reasons. Is there anything else you saw that could put this in context?"

Anya sat silent, lips pressed together, eyes staring up at nothing in particular. "Not really. All the other things, which, by the way, I won't tell you about, seemed very positive as near as I could tell. Stuff about her job and family and the like, but nothing bad."

Jeff tilted his head to the side, pondering. "Well, that doesn't give us a lot to go on, does it? So, what are you looking at from me?"

"Well, I'm not looking for anything, unless there is something you are aware of that could account for this. And the second question is: what should we do about it?"

"Okay, first, I don't have any idea what this could be about. I was worried about Mom for a while after she lost her last job, but she soon found the new one and it seems like she is really interested in it. I heard her on the phone the other day discussing engine displacements and horsepower and gearboxes. She seems to know exactly what she is talking about, which surprised me because she has never been much of a car person. I guess she's getting into it. But you also said it doesn't seem like it was job related, so that throws that idea out the window anyway.

"For your second question, I don't see anything we can do about it. There's not enough information and I don't see any sense in worrying her. That could make it a self-fulfilling prophecy. All I can suggest is that we listen carefully to things she discusses and make sure she's not feeling bad about something that she's not telling us. Does that make sense?"

Anya nodded. "I kind of came to the same conclusion, but she's your mom, so I wanted to talk about it with you."

"Well, I'm glad you did even though you weren't supposed to. I'll keep an eye out, or maybe an ear, in case she hints at any problems or starts feeling mopey with no obvious reason." He leaned over and kissed her lips gently. "Thanks for being concerned."

Anya smiled. "Well, I should be. I'm guessing that someday she'll be my mother-in-law."

CHAPTER 14

About a month later, Anya walked into the apartment and found Jeff putting away stuff from the living room. The smell of onions and potatoes wafted out of the kitchen, so she went there after giving him a brief kiss, and took a deep breath, enjoying the aromas. "Smells really good in here and I'm hungry. What are we having?"

"Steaks, which I need to get going now, and squash and baked potatoes, plus sauteed onions. I hope you're hungry."

"I sure am now. Do I have time for a shower?"

"Sure. This will take me a while, so I won't be able to join you."

She smirked at him. "I think I remember how to do it myself. Is it too early for me to put on my night clothes?"

"Never. I find them tempting."

She turned to walk out of the room. Looking back over her shoulder, she added, "As if I hadn't noticed."

Ten minutes later, Anya returned wearing her deep

pink satiny pajamas which fitted her much better than the clothes Jeff had loaned her before she moved in. He was putting the food on the table as she walked in.

"You look extra lovely tonight." He put his arms around her and briefly kissed her lips.

She shook her head. "You are incorrigible. I know all about your ulterior motives."

"Is that a problem?"

"No, not at all. I will admit that I'm a little surprised that you fixed dinner again this evening."

Jeff tried to look innocent. "Well, with you working late it seems kind of odd to go out afterwards when I can cook."

"What about special occasions, do they work the same way?"

"Like what?"

"My birthday?"

"Sure, we'll go out for that. When is it again?" He paused, looking concerned. "Oh no, it's not today, is it?" He slapped his forehead and jumped up out of his chair, rushing out of the room.

A moment later he came back in with one hand behind his back, now pretending to look sheepish. He placed a medium-sized box next to her like the kind that might hold a man's shirt, wrapped nicely in light pink paper with what looked like a professionally done white bow. He said, "How about if we eat first?"

"You are teasing me, aren't you?" she asked as she ran a finger around the edge of the gold and white bow.

He got a funny grin. "You said you were hungry…"

Anya pressed her lips together and said, "Fine. I can wait." Looking at the table she said, "Don't we get drinks?"

"Oh, almost forgot that too." He got up and pulled a bottle of champagne out of the refrigerator. Setting it on the counter, he pulled off the foil, then removed the cage. Grabbing the cork, he used his other hand to slowly turn the bottle, easing out the cork with a soft pop, then pouring two glasses, one of which he handed to her. "Happy birthday, Anya. I love you."

She started laughing. "You goof. I love you, too." Raising hers up, she clinked glasses with him and took a sip. "Wow. This is really good."

They ate dinner slowly, talking in low voices, but Anya kept glancing over at the box sitting next to her. When Jeff got up to pour them more champagne, she gave the package a shake and heard something shifting around inside.

"Hey, you're not supposed to do that."

She raised her eyebrows and smiled, tilting her head to the side. "Oh? I didn't know that."

By the time they finished, Anya's eyes sparkled and her cheeks were flushed from the alcohol. "So, do I get to open this now?"

"Sure, any time you want."

"That isn't what you implied before…"

"Honey, it's your birthday. You can do anything you want."

She broke out laughing and picked up the package. "You did a nice job with the wrapping."

"Umm, well, the store actually did that, not me. I'm pretty much a fumble-fingers."

"Hmm." She slipped the ribbons off and slowly opened the lid, but all she saw at first was wadded-up tissue paper. Then she noticed the long, thin box that was also wrapped in white tissue so she lifted it out. "A box in a box?"

"Like those Russian nesting dolls."

"Jeff, you know darn well my heritage is Portuguese."

"But I never saw any Portuguese nesting dolls."

"You are hopeless."

"No, mostly English."

Ignoring him, she unwrapped the long box and found a narrow black plush box. Flipping it open, she caught her breath. "Is that a diamond?"

He nodded. "Only the best for you."

"Can we afford it?"

"Yeah. I've been saving up for it."

"Would you put it on me?"

He got up and draped the chain around her neck, fastening the clasp.

"I have to go see this." They went into the bedroom where she admired her reflection in the mirrored closet doors. "This is so beautiful."

Standing behind her, he nibbled on her neck. "It looks especially good on you, though it kind of clashes with the pajamas."

"Do you have a suggestion?"

He unbuttoned the top few buttons of her pajama top, then slid both parts of the pajamas down over her hips into a pink pool on the floor, leaving her naked except for the diamond. "God, you are beautiful."

"We were talking about the necklace."

"That too. And it goes very well with this outfit."

CHAPTER 15

The following Friday, Anya joined the group at Mario's after she'd finished reading palms for the evening. The usual four of them, Jeff, Laura, Marcus, and Karen, had gathered there earlier with the addition of Michael, Karen's new boyfriend.

As soon as she sat down next to Jeff, the waitress came over. Looking at Anya, she asked, "What would you like? We have a new Pinot Grigio that we added to the wine list that is really good. Want to try it?"

Anya paused for a moment, then said, "I'll have an iced tea today. Are you still serving food? I'm hungry."

"The kitchen is open for another two hours. Anybody else want some food?"

Jeff said, "I'll take an order of cheese fries."

As the waitress left, Anya looked at Jeff, raising her eyebrows. "She offered me wine?"

"I think it's the necklace. It makes you look o-l-d-e-r."

Anya and Laura both laughed. "Jeff," Laura said, "I'm guessing our waitress knows how to spell." He shrugged.

"Let us see the necklace." This from Karen. As Anya pulled the lapels on her blouse, Karen and Laura both started oohing and aahing. "Wow, that is so pretty."

A few minutes later the waitress returned with the tea and Anya's salad.

Laura turned to Anya and asked, "I haven't seen you for weeks. How's couple's life working out for the two of you?"

"It's good. We get along well and haven't had any arguments yet. So yeah, really good."

'Well, you need to have at least one argument pretty soon. It's human nature."

Jeff curled the corner of his lip down and looked over at his sister. "Thank you for your insight, oh wise one."

Laura looked back at him and rolled her eyes.

Anya said, "Oh, I suspect we may have one, maybe even pretty soon."

Jeff looked over puzzled. "What don't I know?"

"Oh, we can talk later."

"You're trying to get me worried."

"Not exactly, I wondered if we could get a kitten."

Jeff paused for a moment, blinking. "Oh, you need a

familiar!"

Anya grabbed one of his French fries and threw it at him, hitting his chin. "I read palms. I'm not a witch. Witches are the ones that have familiars"

"I don't know. Your mom threatened to curse me."

"Don't worry, she hasn't figured out how to do that even though she has been trying for years."

That brought a round of laughter from everyone at the table.

Jeff shrugged. "Yeah, we can do that if you want. Maybe it will become *my* familiar. See, there's nothing you can ask for that will bother me. I'm completely unflappable."

Anya gave him a skeptical glance. "Are you absolutely sure about that?"

"Yeah, try me. Anything."

"Maybe later."

"No, go on. Unflappable."

"Okay, I'm pregnant."

Jeff's buddy Marcus said, "Whoa! She got you there!"

Jeff felt everyone's eyes on him watching to see what he would do as he stared at Anya.

"Really?" he asked.

PLEASE, SISTER

Karen said, "You looked pretty flapped."

Anya nodded to him, watching his face.

At first there was a tiny smile while Jeff let it sink in, which expanded into a huge silly grin. "Really?"

Anya smiled. "Yep."

He leaned over to give her a kiss, whispering into her ear. "That's wonderful. I'm so happy."

"I must admit, I've never seen him at a loss of words before," remarked Laura. That got more laughter.

Jeff sat there grinning, his arm around Anya's waist. Looking over at his sister, he said, "Laura, if you tell Mom about this before I do, I'll throw you out my apartment window."

Laura looked confused. "Jeff, you live on the first floor."

CHAPTER 16

Lainie was ecstatic when Jeff and Anya told her they were expecting, and immediately decided they needed to have a party, including Anya's mom, of course. Lainie wanted to meet her anyway, but the opportunity hadn't come up before. She decided on a brunch for the following Sunday morning at her house so Beatriz could get back in time to start her readings.

Laura brought Marcus along while Anya and Jeff brought Beatriz. At first Anya's mom seemed uncomfortable, but she relaxed after her first mimosa, when she and Lainie sat down on the couch and started talking about their kids. Anya declined a mimosa based on her pregnancy, and Jeff declined as a show of support. They sat quietly on the loveseat chatting with Laura and Marcus, who was behaving himself for a change.

Lainie glanced across the room at them. "So, Anya, are you planning to stay in Jeff's apartment with the baby?"

"I think we'll need to get a bigger one. A one-bedroom apartment will get crowded pretty quickly. We were discussing that last night."

"This is a pretty big house. You could move in here if you want."

Jeff groaned, "And live here with Laura? Probably not."

Lainie looked over at her daughter, who spoke up. "Well, no. I'm moving in with Marcus next week, so Mom will be here all by herself."

That surprised Jeff. "Well, congratulations, Sis. I thought that would never happen. I'm so excited for you. Maybe we should order pizza."

Laura laughed. "Okay, okay. I did lay it on a little thick when I found out Anya was moving in with you. I admit it."

Lainie continued, "And really, this place is too big for me. After Laura told me she was moving out, I got to thinking seriously about whether I wanted to stay here by myself. I looked at some nice condos a couple of miles south of here and I love them. I could even sell you the house if you want."

Jeff said, "Hmm ... I'm not sure we're ready to buy a house yet. That's a big step."

Lainie laughed. "In case you hadn't heard, having a baby is a big step too."

They all laughed at that.

"You have no idea. Just wait," added Beatriz.

Lainie added, "I'll even sell it to you for what your Dad and I paid for it."

"Mom, that was what? Twenty-five years ago?"

"Yeah, that's about right."

Jeff shook his head. "Well, that would be great for us but it wouldn't be fair to either you or Laura."

Lainie grinned. "Don't worry. I've already talked to Laura and she's okay with it, and besides, I can afford it. My new job is going really well and I'm making more money than I ever have. So, if you want it, it's yours. But don't ask me to throw in a Corvette."

Jeff looked at Anya, who was sitting there wide-eyed. "We can talk about this later, I guess."

"That is a very generous offer, Ms. Merriwether."

"Oh, Anya, stop calling me that. You can either call me Mom or Lainie." She paused for a moment, perking up, "Or maybe even Grandma! I am so excited about this."

Even the normally dour Beatriz had to smile at this. "Yes, it is certainly exciting. I remember when Tomas and I first got married, and when Anya came along. Those were very happy days." Looking at Lainie, she added, "And now we'll both be grandmothers."

Anya looked across the room at her mother and

smiled. She realized that it was rare that Beatriz seemed this happy, but Anya knew that there had been difficult times after those first few years. Still, it was nice to hear her say that. "Gosh, it seems like everybody's going to be moving all at the same time. Maybe we should buy a moving truck."

"Yeah, or I could buy one and start a side business," commented Marcus.

Laura tilted her head and pursed her lips, staring at him.

He shifted his eyes around the room. Raising his eyebrows, he grinned. "Or not."

CHAPTER 17

Anya, in the middle of painting trim around the ceiling, looked over at Jeff. "This is amazing. Having a baby is wonderful, but I never expected to get our own house so soon."

Jeff looked over at her. "You have yellow paint on your nose."

She giggled and went into the bathroom to wipe it off.

"You're right," he said. "I didn't think we could do that either and here we are painting the baby's room." Pausing again for a moment, he added, "I'm glad that I was able to get out of my lease early so we aren't making two payments at the same time."

Anya nodded. "It's really nice of your mother to offer us this house at the price she did."

"Yeah, I didn't expect that at all. I'm assuming she has something worked out for Laura if they decide to buy, but I haven't heard any details."

"Well, if Laura is okay with this, I guess that's all that matters."

Lainie walked into the room to check on things.

"Wow, this is going quickly with both of you working. When I did stuff like this by myself the trim was dry before I even got to the rollering part. You two make a good team."

"I kind of thought so too," commented Jeff.

"Oh, by the way, I heard from the real estate agent today and they expect the closing on my condo to be next week since there is very little to check on and I'm making a large down payment."

"Will the payments we're making to you cover your payments on the condo?"

"Close enough. Don't worry about it. At least I'll be out of your hair. Oh, and I'm heading over to see how Laura and Marcus are getting settled in. See you later, if you're still up."

"Okay, Mom. Say 'hi' to them for us."

Anya added, "Bye, Mom."

Lainie stuck her head back in the room and gave the girl a big grin before heading for the garage.

"When do you think we'll be done here?" Anya asked. "Soon?"

"I'm thinking about another fifteen minutes and another fifteen to clean up. Did you have something in mind?"

"Well, your mom won't be back for a while, so we

could have some fun, maybe even in the shower."

"Hmm, that sounds like a great idea. How many places in this house are we going to do it?"

"All of them?"

"I'm not sure about that. The attic is pretty grungy. But other than that, I'm game."

Anya giggled again. "Jeff, I love you so much and I'm so happy. I never thought I could feel this way."

He came across the room. "Close your eyes for a moment."

She did. That's when he touched her nose with the roller.

"Eek! What did you do?"

"You have yellow paint on your nose again," he grinned.

She pushed him away. "Oh, go paint the walls." She went back into the bathroom to wipe the paint off.

A short while later they finished painting and Jeff took the roller and brushes to the garage sink to clean up. "I'll be back in a few."

Anya said, "I'm going to hop in the shower."

"Without me?"

"Hurry."

CHAPTER 18

A couple of weeks later, Jeff went over in the early evening to pick up Anya from her palm reading session. The street out front was crowded, so he parked in the alley behind their house.

As he got out of the car, a young man came out in front of him from between two garages. His hands were up in the air and he had no visible weapon. Jeff, standing there with the open car door between them, recognized him: the kid who had tried to rob them a few months ago. "Get out of here. I want nothing to do with you."

Still holding his hands up, the guy replied. "Wait, I want to talk."

"No, I'm not interested in talking to you."

Hearing footsteps behind him, Jeff spun around and saw another man, probably in his late twenties, a few inches taller than Jeff and maybe fifty pounds heavier, but all muscle. "What do you want?" Jeff asked.

This new guy stood about twenty feet away, arms hanging loose at his side, face relaxed and apparently not concerned. He watched Jeff carefully, but again, there was no weapon. "I'm the one who wants to talk to you. And before you do anything stupid, you should know that there are two guns aimed at you right now, so why don't we talk for a few minutes?"

Jeff looked behind him. The younger man now had a pistol aimed at him. Turning back, he said, "I only see one."

"That's intentional. You won't know where the other one is until he kills you, but I'd rather that didn't happen. Either play along or you're dead."

Jeff turned pale as the blood drained from his face, and he felt sweat on his palms, but didn't see a way out of this. "What do you want from me?"

"Willum over there," he said, pointing to the younger man, "told me about an incident from a couple of months ago and I've been looking for you."

"Do you have a name?"

"The only name you need to know is Darius. Now, listen carefully. I have some problems that you can help me with. I'm having difficulty getting some people to pay their bills and do other things they've agreed to do, and you have a way of putting some, shall we say, pressure on them."

Jeff shook his head. "No way, not interested. Leave me alone."

"It wouldn't involve hurting anyone, maybe roughing up some of their stuff so they get the message," Darius continued.

"Why would I ever want to work for you?"

Darius walked closer and put one foot on the rear bumper of Jeff's car, as he nonchalantly pulled out a knife and flipped it open. He began cleaning his fingernails, glancing at Jeff frequently. "Well, for one thing, I pay very well."

Jeff swallowed, confused. "I have a job and I don't need another one. Thanks, but no thanks."

Darius stopped cleaning his fingernails and dropped his arms back to his sides, still holding the knife. "Well, there is one other reason you might consider."

Jeff scanned from side to side, looking for a chance to get away, but with a knife in front of him and a gun or two behind him, the odds weren't good. "What's the reason?"

Darius watched him carefully. "Well, you see, some of my boys have taken an interest in your redheaded girlfriend. They think she might be a lot of fun to play with." He briefly paused, letting it sink in. "In fact, if we give her the right drugs, she wouldn't even know how many of us had her, though I personally think it would be even more fun if she was wide awake the whole time. Who knows, it might take days till we got done with her."

Jeff stared, shaking, unwilling to say anything.

Darius folded his knife and slipped it into his pocket. "On the other hand, I can stop that from happening if you help me out." Again, he paused. "Do you know where the Pigeonhole Bar is over on South Palmer Street?"

Jeff nodded.

"Be there at eight tomorrow night and ask for me … we wouldn't want anything to happen to her, would we?"

With that, Darius turned and walked away. When Jeff looked around, Willum was also gone. He got back in his car and closed the door, shutting his eyes. *How had he gotten into this mess? More importantly, how was he going to get out of it?*

CHAPTER 19

After sitting in the car for a half-hour, Jeff finally stopped shaking, though he was still afraid. He thought he could put up some kind of a front for Anya; there was no way he was going to tell her about the threat. That he would keep to himself.

As he walked into the kitchen, Anya looked up and said, "What's wrong?"

He shook his head. "Oh, it's stuff from work. My boss told me this afternoon that I'm going to have to come in late tomorrow night and get some stuff done. I'm not looking forward to it."

He saw the skepticism on her face, but she said nothing else about it, got up and kissed him and gave him a hug.

Anya shook her head. "Well, if that's the worst that ever happens, I guess it will be okay. Can we go out for dinner tonight? I don't feel like cooking."

Jeff nodded, not trusting himself to look at her. In the back of his mind he imagined what they would do to her if he didn't play along with Darius, at least for a while.

87

After a short discussion, they went back to the Italian restaurant they had gone to before, because that was Anya's preference. This time it was quiet in there, with a dozen or so small groups of people seated around the dining room. Again, they chose to sit in a back corner.

"So, how was your day today, sweetheart?" he asked, trying to seem as normal as possible.

"Umm, it was okay, I guess. We had three people with appointments and another couple of walk-ins. So, it was productive, but not real busy. Tell me about this job you have to do tomorrow night."

"Oh, it's no big deal. Someone gets stuck doing this every couple of months. I guess it's my turn this time."

"How late will you be?"

"Well, I have to go back in around eight in the evening, or maybe I'll hang out at the office and get a jump on things, but there's no way to know how long it will take. I need to clean up some files. If there aren't many, it might only be three to four hours. If there are a lot, I could be there all night. The good part is I get a day off on Monday to compensate."

"So, should I plan on staying home tomorrow to keep you company?" she smiled at him.

"Well, if you want to watch me sleep..."

"That doesn't sound like fun, but if you're up all night I guess you'll need it. Maybe we could do something fun in the evening."

Jeff nodded, "Yeah, that sounds like a good idea, or maybe even in the morning when I get home." He raised his eyebrows and grinned at her.

"Yeah, maybe so."

They chatted for a while, talking about what they wanted to do with the house and, of course, about the baby. They were at odds on whether they wanted to know the gender now, or wait until the child got there. Anya wanted to know, but Jeff was in favor of waiting. Since the room was painted a medium yellow, it didn't make a lot of difference.

After they got home from the restaurant, Anya still seemed remote. Jeff wondered what she was thinking, but didn't want to bring it up.

Anya smiled at him. "You know, I never did get around to reading your palm. How about if I do that for you tonight? Sound like fun?"

Jeff hemmed and hawed. "Why don't we wait until I'm in a better mood? I'm pretty grumpy tonight with this job thing."

Anya turned her head to one side. "Jeff, what is it that you're not telling me? You're never like this. Are you hiding something? Are you having an affair?"

Jeff took her in his arms and gave her a long hug, staring over her shoulder at the wall. "Anya, I would never cheat on you. You are the only one I want for the rest of my life and my goal is to make you happy."

"I'm worried about you, Jeff. You seem distant tonight, ever since you got to my Mom's house this evening. It felt like something was up the minute you walked in the door."

"I know, sweetie. Give me some time to work this out myself, then we can talk about it."

"Is there anything I can do for you?"

Jeff thought about making love to her; he wanted to but the picture that Darius painted popped into his mind and ruined everything. *God, what a mess.*

CHAPTER 20

Jeff went to work as usual Friday morning after dropping Anya off, but he got nothing done all day. Most of the other people in the office were busy, so no one noticed. He was dreading quitting time, watching the clock, worrying about what would come later.

Part of him hoped that it would be no big deal. Maybe all he'd have to do would be to break a few windows, or something like that. If it got worse, well, he'd have to figure that out when he got there, but he wasn't going to start beating people up or killing them. He couldn't. On the other hand, he couldn't risk letting his own secrets get out ... God only knows what would come of that.

When five o'clock got there most of the staff left, but he stayed behind, not wanting to talk to anyone for fear they would know that something was wrong.

A couple hours later, he was about to leave when his boss came out of his office with his coat on, carrying his briefcase. "Hey, Jeff. What are you hanging around for tonight? Behind on stuff?"

"No, not really, Dan. I wanted to wrap up a few things

before I leave."

Dan, a former college quarterback, set his briefcase down. "Are you feeling okay, Jeff? You're white as a ghost."

"Well, I'm under the weather a little. Not sure if it's the flu or a cold. I'm tired and getting stuffy."

Dan looked him over briefly. "Well, you've only taken a couple of sick days since you started here two years ago, I happened to be looking over those numbers today. If you're not feeling better, take Monday off and take it easy. I think we can manage without you for a day or so."

Jeff looked up. "That's nice of you. Maybe I'll do that."

Dan nodded, picking up his briefcase. "Take care of yourself, okay?"

"Will do, boss."

As he watched him walk out the door, Jeff shook his head and finished filing the papers on his desk. There was no reason to go home since Anya was at her mother's house, so he figured he should get some fast food before heading down to the Pigeonhole. He'd driven by the place a few times, but never had any interest in going in … too dark and in an area he didn't like.

He grabbed a burger and some fries on his way, since he figured he needed something to eat, even though that was the last thing on his mind. It was hard forcing it down.

He found the bar with no problem and parked around the corner by the side window rather than right in front. He hesitated for a moment before he got out of his car, and when he thought about Anya, he went in.

It was darker than most bars and seemed smoky, though no one was smoking at that moment. He let his eyes adjust and walked over to the bar counter that ran along one wall of the room.

Before he could say anything, Darius came out of a back room and spotted him. "Hey, man, you're just in time. Want to come in the back room and have a little fun with the guys? We got a hot little chick back there will do anything you like."

"Uh, no thanks. Not interested."

Darius raised his eyebrows. "You're hung up on the redhead bad, man."

"Look, I know I'm a little early, but could we talk business?"

Darius nodded, grinning. "Sure thing." Turning to the bartender, he said, "Colin, get a beer for my new recruit here, and one for me too."

Colin nodded and pulled two glasses from under the counter, filling them from the tap. He handed one glass to Jeff and the other to Darius. There was no mention of payment.

"So, come on over here and we can sit and talk about some stuff. I've got a job I need you to do for me real soon, so you can get your feet wet, ya' know?"

Jeff took a pull on his beer and joined Darius at the table. "Okay, so what do you want done?"

Darius grinned ever wider. "Well, there's this guy that's behind in his payments—owes me over eight thousand dollars and he's missed the last two payments. We need to teach him a lesson."

Jeff took another drink of his beer, hoping it would dull the agony of being here. Suddenly, he knew something was wrong … his head started swimming and even focusing his eyes was difficult. He tried to get up, but he could barely move.

Darius waved two guys over, who helped Jeff up. "Jeff, you take a nice little nap and we'll talk more about this in the morning."

Jeff was barely aware of being carried between the two of them, his feet dragging on the floor.

CHAPTER 21

It was dark. There was a tiny sliver of light coming through a crack under the door, above the floor Jeff was laying on. Concrete. The floor had scratched up his face. His head was throbbing.

After a moment he felt something crawl on his leg. He kicked as hard as he could and heard a thud. Probably a rat, he thought, but he didn't know where he was…

He pushed himself up and noticed that the floor was dirty, grimy. When he got to a sitting position, his head started spinning, but that only lasted a few seconds, so he dragged himself to his feet, stumbling, though he felt very weak.

Thinking back, the bartender—what was his name again?—must have slipped something into his beer. Probably at the request of Darius, but how could he help him when he was stuck down here?

Anya flashed across his mind and he started shaking. They could have lied to him to get to her. Immediately, he shuffled over to where he thought the door was, where he had seen the light. He found it quickly enough and tried the handle … locked, of course.

He felt around and found a light switch and flipped it, but that did nothing. What kind of a room was this, with a door but no windows? Turning back to the door, he felt around the door panel and frame. Both seemed to be made of steel. Hmm, not good. He looked around carefully, trying to see any light sources, but there were none, so he paced along the wall, keeping a hand against it. In four steps he came to an inside corner. Continuing to his left, he got about six steps before he hit the next wall. Eight steps to the next, then six, and three more back to the door. Considering that he had taken small steps, he guessed the room was about eight by ten or so, with only the one door and apparently no windows or other openings.

He shuffled across the floor a few times and didn't run into anything, so this was an empty room, maybe for storage, or for holding people.

His mind was still foggy, but Anya flashed across it again and he knew he had to get out. *Well, there's more than one way to do that.*

He walked to the wall across from the door and could see the tiny sliver of light coming in, so he braced himself with his back against the opposite wall and tried pushing on the door with his mind. It seemed to wiggle a little in the frame, but he had never tried to do anything difficult like this.

Anya. Have to get out. He took all of his attention and focused it on the door, pushing again. It wiggled, stopped, and he strained harder, getting a massive headache in the process, but he didn't care. *Anya.*

The door burst out of its frame and fell into a lit hallway, so he stumbled across and ran out, almost tripping over the frame. There was only one exit and that was to his left, so he went that way, turning a corner and finding another door, but at least there was some light here. He tried the handle and the door opened out.

He was facing three men with guns, and Darius.

"Wondered how long it would take you to get out of there. We heard you moving around about a half-hour ago, so we came down here to wait."

Jeff's anger was off the scale, but he was still facing three guns and a guy who could probably kill him with his bare hands. "What the hell are you doing? Why lock me up?" He clenched his fists, waiting.

"I needed to see if what Willum told me was true, and how strong you are. No more games from me now, I got my answer. You remember I said I had some work for you to do?"

Jeff thought back and vaguely remembered the discussion. He nodded.

"Okay," said Darius, "let's get to work."

Jeff stiffly followed him up the stairs with the three gunmen behind him. Apparently, Darius didn't like taking chances. They came out into the empty bar and Jeff was surprised to see that it was getting light outside.

Willum came in through another door, also carrying a handgun. Darius looked over at him. "You're driving. The two of us will be in the back seat. But keep your gun handy, in case."

Willum nodded and went out the front door to a maroon Ford Taurus right in front of the bar. He got in and started the engine while the two of them climbed in back.

"Where are we going?" Jeff asked.

"Shut up and stop with the questions. You do what I tell you and I'll hold up my end of the deal. Got it?"

Jeff nodded as they started driving. They went about a mile and turned into a residential area. Even though it was light out, after dawn, there was no activity on the street yet. He was watching where they were going when Willum pulled the car over to the curb and stopped, leaving the engine running.

"See that house across the street with the Camry in front of it?"

Jeff looked. It was directly across from him, the windows all still dark. He glanced at Darius and nodded.

"I want you to bust out all of the front windows and the door, then we're gone. Got it?"

Jeff turned back to the house as he rolled down his window.

"Hey, why you doin' that?"

The window down, Jeff turned back to Darius. "You want me to blow out the car window?"

"Huh? No. Go ahead, but no funny stuff."

Jeff focused on the picture window first and it shattered, crashing into the living room. The other three windows came next, about two seconds apart.

The door exploded into the house.

"Willum, get us out of here."

The car burned rubber as they left the neighborhood and headed back to the Pigeonhole.

As they got out, Darius looked at Jeff. "You'll get paid when this guy brings me his money. Now get out of here. Come back Friday night about eight. You even think about calling the cops and you're dead. I have friends there you don't want to mess with. Go!"

CHAPTER 22

"Jeff, you're a mess. What on earth happened to you?"

It was nine in the morning when Jeff got home, still disoriented from the drugs. "I'm okay, Anya, I need a shower and I'll be fine."

She walked closer, to hug him, then looked closely and stopped. "How did you get so filthy? What were you doing?"

He walked over to her and put a hand on each of her arms, holding her away because he was indeed sweaty, filthy, and a little bloody. "Look, we need to talk, but first I need to get a shower. Oh, and could you make me some coffee, that would help."

She nodded at him, but seemed restless and unconvinced. "You want some breakfast, too?"

He gave her a weary grin. "That would be great. Give me about fifteen minutes."

Fifteen minutes later, he came into the kitchen, washed, shaved, and looking more or less normal except for the scratches on his face that had stopped bleeding. "Thanks, hon. I appreciate what you've done here. Let me eat, then we'll talk."

She sat across the table from him and took some scrambled eggs, but nibbled at them, not seeming at all hungry.

When he pushed back his plate, he forced a grin. "Thanks, that was good and I needed it."

"So, do we talk now?"

"Give me your cell phone."

Her eyes went wide. "What? Why?"

He sighed. "Anya, work with me on this. I'm in a difficult situation and I'm trying to make the best of it. Please?"

She handed him her cell phone and he opened a kitchen drawer and put it in there along with his. "We need to keep these somewhere safe, but we can't use them right now and we can't take them with us."

Anya watched him, twisting a strand of her hair between her fingers.

"We're leaving town for a while, and you can tell your Mom, but you can't tell her where we're going."

"Are you going to tell me?"

"Look, Anya, there's a lot of reasons to leave now, but one thing you must know is that I love you and want to keep you safe. I want to elope with you, today, and find someplace to get married. Nobody but the two of us. Anya, I love you so much, but I also need to get out of town for a while. Can you live with that for now?"

"Obviously, there is a lot more to this story. When do I hear that part?"

"After we get where we're going, I'll tell you everything and answer all your questions. But first, we need to leave."

"Okay, when?"

"One hour. Let's get packing."

She sat up straight, eyes widening. "Are you in trouble?"

"Yes. Big time. More on that later. Let's go. You can tell your Mom that we're eloping, but not where or when we'll be back." He paused for a moment, watching her face. "I hate to do this to you, but we have to. Can you just trust me for a few days?"

She bit her lip for a moment, something he had never seen her do before, but this was an unusual circumstance and they were both under stress.

"Yes. Of course. I'm with you regardless. I'll go pack my stuff. Are we driving?"

"Yep. Wish my Mom had given me a Corvette along

with the house, we could have taken that."

She turned down one side of her mouth, raising her eyebrows. "At least you still have a sense of humor, even if it's bad."

He winked at her, confusing her even further, but she got up and went to pack.

CHAPTER 23

Two days of driving found them in Carson City, Nevada. Both were exhausted though they had taken turns driving, only stopping for food and gas, sleeping while the other one drove. Jeff had refused to discuss the reason for the trip with Anya, who was angry and spent much of the trip alternating between frustration and pouting, with occasional outbursts at him.

They found an inexpensive motel that seemed clean, and Jeff paid for several nights in cash. Anya raised her eyebrows at this, but said nothing.

Once in their room, they threw their luggage onto the bed and went out for a late lunch so they could spend the rest of the day getting back to normal.

After finishing the meal, they came back and Jeff sat on the bed, so Anya sat in the chair by the desk, still angry.

"Jeff, *now* will you tell me what this is all about? And don't say you wanted to elope. I'm not buying that after you insist on paying cash for the room, the gas and our meals."

Jeff sat facing her, his back against the headboard.

He nodded. "Yes, I will. I wanted to do this when we were not distracted and I'd had time to think it through."

Anya nodded, watching him carefully.

He continued, "Do you remember when the kid tried to rob us in the alley, several months back?"

"Well, sure. You knocked him over and he ran off without his knife."

"Yep. Apparently, that wasn't the end of the story. He told his boss about it and the boss decided he wanted me to work for him. As an enforcer, I guess, busting up people's property if they didn't pay him back on time. He threatened me and said I would regret it if I didn't play along."

"Okay, so you should have gone to the police. They would have taken care of it. Did you?"

Jeff let out a long sigh and shook his head. "It's not that simple. Here's how it happened. The kid who tried to rob us, Willum, popped out in front of me when I was getting out of the car. He didn't have any weapons that I could see, so I told him to go away, that I wanted nothing to do with him.

"Then this big, muscular guy showed up and told me there were two guns aimed at me so I shouldn't, as he put it, 'do anything stupid.'

"He told me what he wanted and I said no, to leave

me alone, but he insisted. Then he said one other thing that stopped me cold.

"He said some of his boys were interested in you, and if I didn't play along, they were going to gang-rape you."

Anya sat silent, eyes getting wider, her normally pale skin fading to paper white.

"Anya, it wasn't an empty threat. I would do anything to keep you safe."

She got up from the chair and came over to sit next to him on the bed. Jeff put his arm around her and felt her shaking. He held her for a long time. For most of it she cried.

After a while, he got her some tissues and she wiped her face. Finally, after taking some deep breaths, she blew her nose and looked at him, still terrified. "What about the police, can we go to them?"

"I went over to a bar to meet with Darius—he's the leader—thinking it was just to talk. I'm sorry I lied to you about where I was going."

She nodded. "Go on."

"From some conversation I caught bits of, there is a police captain who likes to play along with them when they kidnap a girl ... likes to be the first one and makes sure they aren't drugged, so they're aware of the whole damn thing. A lot of the women seem to wind up in the river."

Anya shivered again, but forced herself to calm down.

"When I got there to talk with Darius, he told the bartender to give each of us a beer. We went over to a table to talk. Apparently, mine was drugged.

"The next morning, I woke up in an empty locked room, in the dark, lying on a concrete floor. When I finally gathered my wits about me, I blew the door off its hinges. Darius was waiting for me with three guys with guns.

"He took me over to someone's house and stopped out front, told me to blow out the windows and front door. I did. Then he told me to go home and come back next Friday."

He shook his head. "Anya, I don't know how to get out of this. I need to protect you and our baby. I don't know who to trust and don't even care what happens to me as long as I know you'll be safe."

"Jeff, wait. Don't talk like that. We're in this together and we'll get out of it together."

He shook his head and buried his face in his hands. "Why was I so stupid when Willum tried to rob us? We could have given him our money and none of this would have happened."

"Jeff, stop it. You kept us from getting robbed. There was no way you could have known about the outcome. Let's focus on what we can do now."

"Anya, I'm scared, for both of us."

"Me too. And I don't know what to do right now either." She paused for a few moments. "Look, I'm sorry I gave you a hard time on the drive out here. I had no idea…"

"It's okay. There was a lot I wasn't telling you."

"Jeff, I have a question. Who else knows about your abilities besides me and Darius?"

"Well, Willum knows for sure. And like I told you a couple of weeks ago, Laura found out, but she's sworn to silence. She's afraid I'll drop her on the couch again."

For some reason, in the midst of all this pain, both of them laughed uncontrollably.

CHAPTER 24

The following day was a Tuesday, so Jeff and Anya went to the Carson City courthouse and, after standing in line for an hour and filling out forms, got a marriage license. The other people in line all seemed so happy, but he couldn't feel that way right now, even though this was what he wanted. There was considerable discussion the prior evening. Love was not the issue, or their desire to be married, but the questions all had to do with the circumstances they found themselves in. They finally decided that this was what they both wanted, regardless, and they would figure out the rest later.

They filled out the paperwork feeling both excited and distraught. But there was nothing to be done for their circumstances right now, so they put it aside.

Later that day, license in hand, they went to a wedding chapel that had been recommended by the owner of the motel they were staying in, an elderly woman whose husband had died several years earlier, leaving her to care for the property by herself.

They were hesitant about the place at first, since the motel woman seemed a little odd, but it turned out to be a good suggestion. The chapel had an antique ambiance that suited their mood well … they wished they were back in a simpler time. For this, Jeff had to use his credit card, crossing his fingers as it was run through the machine, but he was running out of the cash he had taken out of the bank before they left. They got several sets of pictures printed which were ready for them about an hour after the ceremony … enough time for a quiet dinner at a nearby restaurant. Then they went back to the motel, happy about the wedding, but unsure of what the future would bring.

"Maybe I could find a job out here? How would you feel about that?" Jeff asked.

"I don't care where we are as long as we're together, but what do we do when they find us? We can't keep running."

"They can't keep looking for us forever."

"But what about the police captain? Would he have a way to track us?" asked Anya.

"I don't know. I can't be that important to them. It's not like I've done much for them. Maybe they'll give up," said Jeff. Anya still frowned, and Jeff was worried, though he tried to present a good front for her.

"Well, if nothing else, they could track us here from the pictures we sent to our Moms this afternoon, though those will take a few days to get there," she replied. "Perhaps we should have waited with those."

"Maybe something will come up tomorrow," he replied, opening a bottle of champagne that they had bought for the occasion. He poured some into the two plastic flutes they had also bought. It was a small, private celebration, but it was all they had.

The following morning, Anya got up first and took a shower, letting Jeff sleep in. By the time she came out of the bathroom, however, he was sitting up in bed, waiting for her. "I guess we should at least call our parents and let them know we're okay, even if we don't tell them where we are," he said.

"Hmm, good idea. Can we use our cell phones, you think?"

"They're still in the drawer at home. Let's see if we can find a pay phone around here, though I'm not sure if that would be any better."

Anya nodded as Jeff went to take a shower.

Forty-five minutes later they had finished a large breakfast in a local casino and were feeling a little better.

Anya asked, "So who goes first? You want to call your Mom, or should I call mine?"

"You go first, then I'll call my mom."

The phone booth in the lobby was not in use, so Anya went in to call. Jeff stood by, watching her, listening.

"Who is this?" Anya asked, raising Jeff's concern.

"Oh, Aunt Maria. This is Anya. Are you over visiting my Mom?"

There was a long pause while she listened to the response, eyebrows drawing closer together, turning to the wall to block out the noise of people passing by.

"How is she doing?"

Another long pause. Jeff, watching, was growing ever more concerned. This was not the conversation he had been expecting.

"How long will she be there?"

A shorter pause.

"Okay, I'll get there as soon as I can."

Jeff's eyebrows went up when Anya said this, hanging up the phone. As she turned back to him, he saw her face wet with tears, shaking.

"My Mom was beat up this morning. She has a broken arm and is in the hospital but should be okay. Aunt Maria is with her. The house was trashed, too."

Jeff took her in his arms, not even bothering to ask who would have done this. "Anya, I never thought…"

"Hush. I know. It's not your fault."

Pulling her tight, he buried his face in her shoulder. "Oh, shit."

CHAPTER 25

The drive back from Nevada was much like the one out, only in reverse. They took turns driving with minimal stops; the only difference was that they were using credit cards again, since it didn't seem to matter anymore.

When they got back, they drove directly to the hospital, but Anya's Mom had already been released. Anya called her Mom's cell phone and found that she her and her sister Maria were at the house/parlor on Claire Street, trying to get things cleaned up, so they went there.

As they walked into the front room, they saw lamps and decorations broken and strewn around the room. Two of the chairs were lying sideways, also broken. The sofa had been slashed beyond all recognition.

Walking into the next room, they found the two women picking up more trashed chairs, Beatriz using only her good arm while the other was in a cast. Anya immediately went to hug her mother and as she did, Jeff saw the older woman glaring at him over her daughter's shoulder.

"You were right, Mom. I've made a mess of

everything," he said.

She continued to glare at him for a moment before her face softened and she walked over to give him a hug also. "We have some work to do, huh?"

He nodded, not entirely sure what that meant, saying nothing more.

Anya wanted to stay and clean up, but Jeff was having none of it. "You can't stay here, not now at least. I have to go see someone to get this sorted out and I want you somewhere they won't suspect until I do that."

Anya reluctantly agreed, turning to her Mom. "I'll be back as soon as I can."

Beatriz nodded and watched them leave.

Their next stop was at his Mom's new condo which was a few miles away, and someplace they hoped wasn't being watched.

"Jeff, Anya, I'm glad to see you're back," she said, giving each of them a hug and patting Anya's stomach. "Baby Merriwether still doing okay?"

"Getting bigger by the day," replied Anya with a grin.

"Do you know the baby's gender yet?"

Jeff shrugged, "No, we're still discussing that point."

"Let me guess, she wants to know and you don't?"

He nodded.

"You're like your father, he always wanted to wait until you kids got here." She waited for a moment. "I heard what happened to Beatriz. How is she doing?"

Anya said, "She's back home now and my aunt is helping her clean up the mess."

"Do the police have any idea who did this, or why?"

Jeff looked at his shoes for a moment. "No, they didn't file a report."

Lainie blinked for a second and sat down in an armchair. "Okay … why don't you two sit down and tell me how much trouble you're in, since it seems you already know the answer to who did this?"

They did sit down, but Jeff was at a loss for what to say. "Mom, it's nothing. Leave it alone."

"Jeff, I'm trying to help."

"Mom, I need you to stay out of this."

"Jeff," Lainie looked at him, "do you need money?"

He shook his head. "I wish it was that simple."

Lainie sat there, staring at both of them.

Anya looked at him. "Show her."

Jeff snapped his head around to look at her. "No!"

"Go ahead, Jeff, she's your mother. She deserves to know."

He shrugged slowly. "Are you sure, Anya?"

"Yes, do it."

Jeff turned to look at his Mom and lifted her off the chair and dropped her from about three inches.

Lainie's eyes popped wide and her chin trembled as she stared at her son, speechless.

To confirm the point, Jeff picked up the other armchair and moved it two feet, setting it down gently.

Getting control of herself, Lainie said, "Oh my God. That's you?"

He nodded. "Don't tell anyone else. Laura already knows, but absolutely no one else."

"Except for a couple of people we wish didn't know," appended Anya.

Lainie paused for a moment, considering. "Are they the ones behind all this?" asked Lainie.

"I'd bet on it," Jeff replied. "Look, I didn't want to get you involved in this, but could Anya stay here for a while? I need to go see someone."

His mother asked, "Is it safe?"

Jeff stalled for a few seconds. "Probably not, but I have to do it anyway."

Frowning, Lainie nodded.

Even though the condo was a little further away, the drive down to the Pigeonhole didn't take long. When Jeff walked in the door, he saw a lot of people in business attire that he didn't recognize having lunch. It was not what he expected.

Colin was behind the bar again, though, so he took a seat there and ordered a beer, wondering if he was risking another drugging.

As he put it in front of Jeff, Colin said, "This is a regular one. Sorry about the other night. Sometimes you have to do things you don't want to do."

Jeff took a sip of his beer and nodded. "Yeah, I get that. Is Darius around?"

"No, but he'll be here later."

"Tell him I'll see him around eight o'clock."

Colin nodded. "The beer is on the house."

CHAPTER 26

At eight that evening, Jeff walked into the Pigeonhole and after his eyes adjusted to the dim light, he spotted Darius, who was in a conversation with some people Jeff didn't know. One of the other guys nudged Darius on the arm and pointed his thumb in Jeff's direction.

"Jeff," Darius said, "I see you're back. Let me introduce you to someone." Taking him over to a uniformed police officer, he said, "This is Captain Brady of the Municipal Police Department. He's a friend of ours."

Brady didn't offer his hand to shake, so Jeff nodded to the man.

Continuing, Darius said, "Let's go in the back room. There are some things we should talk about."

Wary, Jeff nodded and followed the two of them.

Darius again took the lead. "How was Nevada? You have a nice trip?"

"Umm, yeah, it was okay," Jeff replied.

"So, look here. If you do something like that again, all

119

bets are off and we'll work without you. You get it?"

Jeff nodded.

Brady said, "I had to pull in some favors at the department to get you tracked. License plate cameras are common on Highway Patrol cars these days and several of them picked you up on the way. We can find you … anywhere. Don't make us do it again or I'll be really pissed and all agreements are off."

Jeff again nodded, and Brady turned to go. Then he spun around and slammed his fist into Jeff's kidneys.

Jeff crumpled to the floor, moaning, unable to say anything. He looked up at Brady.

"By the way, I'm hoping you do something stupid. I really like that little girlfriend of yours. I bet she'd put up a good fight," he sneered as he walked away.

Darius kicked him in the shoulder, knocking him from his knees to his back. "You don't get any more mistakes. One stupid move and you wind up in the river."

Jeff rolled over and tried to get up, but the pain kept him down.

"We've got work to do. You've got five minutes," Darius said, walking away.

A few minutes later, still bent over in pain, Jeff

staggered into the main room of the bar and over to Darius. "I'm ready when you are."

"You're looking a little white, dude, but it's good that you're paying attention." Motioning to Willum, Darius said, "Bring the car around, we're going for a drive."

A minute later, Willum pulled up in the same maroon Taurus they used before and Darius grabbed Jeff by the arm, dragging him outside, oblivious to his pain, and went around the other side, leaving Jeff to fend for himself with the door.

Knowing he had pushed boundaries already, Jeff got in and sat down. He didn't ask questions this time, just watched as he tracked the path Willum was driving.

They came to a stop in a nicer neighborhood than the prior time, in front of a brick bungalow with a police car sitting in the front.

Jeff looked at Darius, a question in his eyes.

"This guy is not one of our favorite cops. Flip his car over and we'll get out of here," instructed Darius,

Jeff rolled down the window. It took him about three seconds to flip the car, which immediately set off an alarm.

"Go, Willum. Get us out of here," shouted Darius.

Willum did, this time driving fast without the noise of

squealing tires.

"It's time to dump this car. Pull the plates and get rid of them. Take the car somewhere and torch it. Don't get caught," Darius directed.

Willum nodded, dropped them off at the bar and went to dispose of the car.

CHAPTER 27

Anya looked up as Jeff walked in the door. "Well, at least you're not beat up like last time."

Jeff tried to grin, but he was still in pain. "My kidneys are still a little sore, but that should wear off by morning," he shrugged, "I hope."

Anya shook her head. "Jeff, we can't keep going like this. You'll be dead in a month at this rate."

"No, I won't. I have to learn how to play the game so they leave me alone ... I have to stop fighting them." He paused for a few seconds. "Thinking about it, that may be what they want, for me to fight them so they have an excuse. If I go along, maybe I'll be okay."

"For how long?" she asked.

"I wish I knew the answer to that. Maybe I can fake it for a while, pretend I'm okay with it, not cause trouble."

Anya shrugged, saying nothing.

"Oh, by the way," he handed her an envelope, "apparently the first guy whose house I attacked paid out his loan. There's a thousand dollars in there. Give

123

it to your mother … she deserves it."

"Jeff, I don't want to use this to help my Mom."

He stared at her for a moment. "Anya, it's money. I can't turn it down without causing more trouble and I'm not going to do that. Maybe she can buy new furniture to make up for what was destroyed."

"But this is dirty money. She won't want it."

Tired and still in pain, he shook his head. "Anya, money is money, regardless of where it comes from. There's no such thing as good money or bad money, it just is. Tell her I had it saved up. I don't care what you tell her. She should take it."

"Jeff, I'm worried about you."

He nodded. "So am I. But not as much as I'm worried about you and our child."

Anya shook her head, distraught. "Jeff…"

"Yeah, I know, hon. There's no good solution." He took her in his arms and held her for a long time as she cried, then finally stopped.

"Anya, I don't know what else to do. I'm trying to make the best of this but I don't know how. In fact, I don't even have a clue.

"Part of me wants to kill all the bad guys and run away, but that's a fantasy. I don't see any reality that works for us and it scares me to death."

"I know," she sobbed. "It's so confusing and unfair."

"Yeah, you're right. Oscar Wilde said 'life is never fair,' but I doubt that he had this kind of situation in mind. Or maybe he did."

Anya said nothing, sobbing in his arms.

"I'd like to get your Mom out of their reach. Has she ever considered moving? Would she be willing to move in here with us? She could help with the baby when it comes…"

Anya looked up, startled. "Why would you want to do that?"

He shook his head. "To put her a little further away from them. At least there are some neighbors here who would call the cops if they saw something strange."

"But she's still mad at you."

Jeff nodded. "I don't blame her. But it might be best for all of us."

Anya stared at him, incredulous. "Would you be willing to do that?"

He frowned, surprised at the question. "Of course. I'm the one causing the problems. Why wouldn't I do something to fix it?"

"You are not the one causing the problem, it's them."

"Well, yeah, but it's because of me."

"Jeff, you are not responsible for this, not at all."

He shrugged. "That doesn't mean I can't do something to remedy it, or at least try."

"Are you always this nice?"

"Anya, I'm not being nice. It's the best thing. It's logic or … shit, I don't know what it is."

CHAPTER 28

Marcus and Laura showed up at the house unexpectedly. Not that they needed an invitation, it just surprised Jeff and Anya.

"Anya, how is the baby doing? Are you feeling okay?" asked Laura.

'Yeah, I'm feeling a lot better since the morning sickness went away. I've got more energy and I'm anxious to get things ready for the baby. I got the baby's room painted, with some help from Jeff when he wasn't goofing around."

"So you're ready … well, as much as you can be?"

"We still need a crib and some other stuff, but the biggest part is done."

"Show me. This is so exciting." With that, the two girls went up the stairs to look at the nursery.

"So how are you and my sister getting along in the same apartment?" Jeff asked Marcus.

"Oh, we're doing okay. It takes a bit of adjustment, but we expected that." Marcus replied.

"Anya says she keeps getting bigger. I have to tell her she's not starting to waddle, she just walks a little more carefully than she did," Jeff said. "What brings you guys by tonight, anything special?"

Marcus shook his head. "Nope. Wanted to see what you're doing with the house and the baby's room. Is it a boy or a girl?"

Jeff grinned. "Yes, definitely one of those," he said as he handed his buddy a beer from the refrigerator.

Marcus shook his head. "You don't know yet? I would have wanted to know immediately, if not sooner."

"Doesn't work that way," Jeff said.

"You know, there is something I wanted to ask you about, now that the girls are out of here," Marcus said.

Taking a sip of beer, Jeff said, "Yeah. What's up?"

"Well Laura was in a funky mood the other day and I asked her about it. She said she was worried about you. What's going on? Having problems?"

Jeff shook his head. "No, we're doing fine. Waiting for the baby to pop out, though, that's still a ways down the road. Don't know why she would be concerned."

Marcus stared at him. "So why don't I believe that? Are you in some kind of trouble? Maybe something you don't want Anya to know about?"

"Marcus, Anya knows everything that I know. I try to make sure of that. That should be a lesson for you."

"Well, what was the deal with the sudden elopement? I was looking forward to being your best man or something."

"You know," Jeff replied, "weddings are expensive and a really big deal and we didn't want to go through the hassle. Yeah, it was sudden, but that way nobody could try to talk us out of it. We wanted it to be the two of us."

"So you went to Vegas?"

"Well, Nevada, but not Vegas, that's too glitzy for our tastes. But now we're happily married and things are good."

Marcus frowned. "Seems odd that Laura would be worried. No medical problems, money problems? You know I'll help you any way I can. All you have to do is ask."

Lots of thoughts spun through Jeff's mind, but getting someone else involved in their problems would be a total disaster, putting that person at risk also, and he knew it. "Man, everything is good. Laura is paranoid. Haven't you figured that out yet?"

Marcus chuckled. "She does seem that way at times, but she's right more often than wrong. If anything does come up, let me know. I'm here to help."

"Thanks, Marcus, I'll keep that in mind." Jeff took a swig of beer. "Want to see the baby's room?"

"It's not contagious, is it?"

CHAPTER 29

Jeff came home late a few weeks later with his shirt covered in blood from his shoulder.

"My God, Jeff, what happened?" asked Anya.

"We did a break-in at a small shop to steal stuff. Unfortunately, the owner lived upstairs and two of us were shot before we could get out of there."

"I'll put my shoes on and take you to the hospital. Give me a minute."

"Anya, stop. We can't go to the hospital. This is obviously a gunshot wound and they would have to report it to the police. I can't have that. Anyway, it was a .22 that he used and the bullet went all the way through. It's a flesh wound, so it should be fine. I need you to patch it up and I need to get hold of some antibiotics."

Anya paused, staring at him.

"Oh, and I guess I'll need a sling for a while," he added.

"Jeff, you can't let this go..."

He shook his head. "It's a muscle wound, not the joint." Pausing for a moment, he said, "Think about it, Anya. I have to." He saw the tears in her eyes and tried to interrupt it. "Can you cry *after* you patch this up?"

Anya shook her head, clearing it. "Yeah, sorry. What do you want me to do?"

"Clean the entry and exit wounds and patch them up with some gauze and tape, then find me some pain-killers and antibiotics."

As they climbed the stairs, Anya commented, "I have some antibiotics from when I got pneumonia a year or so ago—didn't take the last of them."

Holding his right arm tight against his chest with his left as he walked in to the bathroom, he said, "Yeah, that should be good. And if we don't have anything better, I can take ibuprofen for the pain."

He sat on the toilet lid. Anya, taking great care, peeled the shirt back from the front before deciding to cut the whole thing off, which she proceeded to do. "Well, it's still bleeding a little on both sides. How do I stop it?"

"Clean it up first, since that will probably make it bleed more. We can put some temporary bandages on until it stops." Pulling an antiseptic cream out of the drawer, he handed it to her. "Put some of this on the bandages before you put them on. Maybe it won't stick to the wound that way." He thought for a moment, "Come to think of it, give me some of the ibuprofen first so it starts to kick in."

Anya handed him two ibuprofen tablets and set the glass of water on the sink. "You want more than this?"

"Yeah, give me one more to start out."

She did, but watched him very closely, noticing him wince as he swallowed the pills. "You're looking pale. Are you okay?"

He looked sideways at her, pursing his lips. "No, I've been shot."

She pursed her lips. "You can't be too bad if you're being a smart-ass."

He looked at the ceiling. "Fix me, please?"

Anya cleaned both sides of his shoulder with peroxide while he sat there grimacing. She patched it up with gauze pads and tape and rigged up a sling from some old tee-shirts they planned to throw away. "Well, it doesn't look too bad from what I could tell, and it doesn't seem to be bleeding much anymore. How do you know how to do this?"

"I'm a guy. Getting hurt is part of the deal. I watched my Mom fix me up. Even had to do it myself a couple of times."

"How does it feel?"

"It hurts like hell, but I think I'll live, so I can annoy you for a long time. Haven't been able to do enough of that yet."

"Jeff, are you ever serious?"

CHAPTER 30

A few days later, after Anya arrived at her mother's house, she said, "Mom, why don't you want to move in with us? You can help with the baby when it gets here and you'll be safer there than you are here."

Beatriz crossed her arms over her chest. "I've been here for 32 years. Why should I move now?"

"Well, let's start with the house getting trashed and you getting your arm broken." Frustrated, Anya added, "They know where you live now."

"Yes. Well, how do they know where I live?"

Before she even thought about it, Anya said, "Because they knew where I lived."

Beatriz blinked. "You're part of this too?"

"No, of course not. Jeff is the only one doing anything with this group of thugs. I have nothing to do with it."

"Anya, I know these kinds of people. I've seen them before. Why is Jeff doing this? Can't he go to the police?"

"No, Mom, one of the police captains is part of this

group. He's the one who tracked us to Nevada. I guess when they saw we had run away, they came after you as a lesson."

"Anya, this sounds like your father. Does Jeff owe them money?"

"No, he doesn't. They're paying him when he helps, but he's afraid to turn down the money because they'll suspect he's up to something. So, he's playing along for now, trying to find a way out."

"And what happens if he doesn't play?"

"They'll kill him. I can't let that happen."

"Anya, there's something you're not telling me. I can tell. What is it? And why do they care where you live?"

Anya slowly turned pale, starting to cry, shaking her head.

Beatriz watched for a moment then put her good arm around her daughter. "What else? Tell me."

"Jeff is … is doing it to … protect me," she stammered between sobs.

"They want to kill you?"

Anya shook her head. "No, worse."

Beatriz's eyes got wider. "Oh my God. They want to rape you?"

Anya nodded, sobbing harder. "All of them—Jeff is the only thing stopping them. If he quits, they come for me."

"Jesus!" Beatriz stared at her daughter while she thought this through. "Is that the only reason Jeff is doing this?"

Anya nodded. She'd already told her mother far more than she ever intended and she was afraid to say anything else. If her Mom knew what Jeff had gone through, the beatings, the gunshot…"

Beatriz coaxed her daughter onto a kitchen chair and stood there with an arm around Anya's shoulder while the younger woman cried.

A short while later, Beatriz asked, "Does Jeff know you want me to move in with you two?"

Anya nodded, still sniffling, and drying her eyes. "He was the one who suggested it."

Beatriz stopped for a moment, her mouth open. "*He* said that? I didn't think he liked me at all."

"Mom, it's not that. He understands that you're worried about me and he doesn't hold it against you. I think you could get to like him if you gave him a chance."

"I see. Apparently, I've been wrong about him since we first met."

Anya nodded. She bit her tongue to keep from saying *I told you so.*

CHAPTER 31

"So, what did you do to your arm?" Marcus asked.

The group of friends was back in Mario's Bar and Grill on a Friday night, like old times, except with Anya and also Karen's boyfriend Michael there, too.

"Oh, some of the guys at work decided they wanted to play rugby, and they talked me into joining them. It was okay until I took a hit that slammed my shoulder into the ground. It will heal eventually," Jeff replied.

Skeptically, Marcus asked, "Is that why it's bleeding through your shirt?"

"Oh, crap. I thought it had stopped doing that. Yeah, it got scratched up pretty bad and Anya had to patch me up. Good thing she's not queasy."

"Who says I'm not?" Anya asked. "I almost threw up when I saw it."

"Nonetheless, you got it patched up and it will be fine in a couple of weeks," Jeff responded.

"Is this like what happened when we were playing touch football in college?" asked Marcus.

Jeff nodded. "Yep. Same shoulder too. I think I need to learn to fall down better."

"Or maybe not fall down at all? And stop doing stupid things?" Marcus asked.

"I'm not sure you're one to talk after some of the stuff you did, like that second-floor balcony stunt in college that broke your leg," replied Jeff.

Marcus grinned. "At least the girl came home with me after a few days…"

Laura shook her head. "Enough of this macho stuff. Can we talk about something else?"

Marcus nodded his head. "Yeah, what are we drinking?"

Laura put her face down into her hands, covering it. "Hopeless. You're both hopeless."

Anya laughed. "Well, I know what I'm drinking. I'm having a soda and a tiny sip of whatever Jeff is having."

Karen looked at her. "Anya, you're cheating. We've never even seen you drunk."

Anya shook her head. "Blame Jeff, he's the one who got me pregnant. Believe me, I was looking forward to wine and fizzy girl-drinks, but he ruined it!"

That got another round of laughter as the waitress came up for their order.

"So, what's it going to be, Karen? You seem to like deciding for us all the time," quipped Jeff.

Karen thought for a moment. "We're going to do something different tonight." The whole group groaned. "You can drink whatever you like."

Four of them cheered, high-fiving each other while the waitress gaped at them.

Jeff took the lead. "Give me a bourbon and soda."

"Beer for me," said Marcus.

"Make that two," added Michael.

"Get me a lemon-lime soda," said Anya,

Laura shrugged. "Gin and tonic for me."

"Wait," said Jeff, "have you ever had a gin and tonic before?"

She puckered her lips before answering. "No. I'm trying something new for a change."

Karen looked around. "Well, this is different. I'll have a gin and tonic, too."

Laura and Karen looked at each other and shook their heads. It promised to be a long night.

As the waitress departed, Michael asked, "So how are things in baby-ville?"

"Pink," said Anya.

"A girl? Really?" asked Karen.

"Or blue," added Jeff.

Michael looked from one to the other. "I take it you don't know yet."

Raising her nose very high, Anya said, "I don't want to discuss that subject anymore."

"Better be careful," Michael added, "you might get one of each."

Jeff scowled at him. "Begone, evil spirit."

That brought more laughter as the waitress showed up with a tray of drinks.

CHAPTER 32

"Jeff, I think you should see a doctor about that shoulder. It should be better by now, and it still bleeds occasionally. It's been two weeks since you were shot."

As he struggled to put on his shirt, Jeff said, "Anya, I can't. We've had this discussion before. There's damage all the way through the shoulder, so it will take time to heal. If I went to a doctor, he'd want MRIs and X-rays and all sorts of stuff, and he'd turn it in to the police as a bullet wound."

"But we're out of my antibiotics and it's still causing problems."

"Let me see if I can get some another way,"

Anya shook her head. "I don't like the sound of that. What are you thinking?"

"Anya, you worry too much. Give me a few days to try something else."

"You're going to talk to Darius about this, aren't you?"

"Do you have a better suggestion?"

Anya frowned. "Well, no. I suppose I could pretend to be sick…"

"You're pregnant. They wouldn't want to give you antibiotics anyway."

"Maybe your Mom, or Laura, or even my Mom?"

"Anya, wait until tomorrow and let me see if I can figure this out."

"Fine," she replied, pursing her lips, "do it your way."

"Sweetheart, what's been bothering you lately? You seem so uptight all the time."

Anya frowned, shaking her head. "Don't worry about it."

"Anya…" He paused, waiting for her.

"It's that we never seem to have much time together, and when we do, you're so distracted. It's like you're not even there."

Jeff put his good arm around her shoulder and pulled her close. "I know. I'm sorry, really. Did you have something in mind?" he said, raising his eyebrows.

She grinned a little, trying to hide it. "Well, maybe."

"Hmm, I see," he responded, starting to nibble on her earlobe. "Well it has been quite a while since we tried that."

PLEASE, SISTER

"What about your shoulder? Can you?"

"Don't ask me to hold you up in the shower again for a few more weeks, but I think we could work out something. Maybe even in the baby's room."

"Well, that would be appropriate, wouldn't it? And with the crib mattress still lying on the floor, it might even be comfortable." She paused. "But I'm afraid it will hurt you."

"I think I can handle it. Ignore it when I start moaning."

"You mean like you do all the time?" she asked.

"Yeah, like that."

CHAPTER 33

The Pigeonhole was crowded with Darius' 'associates' when Jeff walked into the bar the next evening. It was only seven o'clock, so he was earlier than usual.

"Jeff, glad to see you're here. We have some work to do a little later tonight. How's that shoulder doing?" Darius said.

"Hey, Darius. It's still giving me a little trouble and I've run out of antibiotics for it."

"I have just the thing for you, then." Leading Jeff back outside the front door, Darius pointed south. "There's a little pharmacy two blocks down on the right side, Andre's." Darius glanced at his watch, "He's still open for another hour and we're not leaving for a while. Run down there and tell him I sent you. Be discreet."

Jeff nodded. "Got it. Be back in a few."

It was an easy walk down and the weather had turned nice, so Jeff enjoyed the diversion. He found the store and went in, but another customer was being helped, so he looked around, and picked up a bottle of ibuprofen since he was running low on that, too. When the other customer left, Jeff went up to the counter.

The pharmacist was a thin, older man with thick gray hair and a pleasant smile. "What can I do for you this evening, young man?"

Jeff glanced around to make sure they were alone. "Are you Andre?" When the older man nodded, he continued. "Darius said you might be able to help me with some antibiotics for my shoulder."

Andre nodded. "You must be the other one that got shot. Had to do this for your partner, too. Though you don't look the part."

Jeff shrugged, at a loss for what to say. Andre went into the back room for a few minutes, and came back out with a pill bottle with no label and handed it to Jeff. "Take one of these twice a day, with a meal. You probably won't need all of them but take them anyway to be sure ... should take about a week to clear up any infection. If you have questions, come back in."

Jeff handed him the ibuprofen and Andre put both bottles in a bag and handed it back to him.

"How much do I owe you?"

Andre looked surprised. "Nothing. Don't tell anyone where these came from. Darius keeps me on retainer for cases like this."

Jeff nodded. "Well, thanks."

As he walked back to the bar, Jeff thought about the situation he was in. In some ways, it was like a normal job—apparently, he even had benefits. The only catch was that he was a criminal. *How very strange.*

When he entered the Pigeonhole, things were pretty quiet and Darius didn't seem to be around at that moment. Jeff ordered a burger and a beer, and took one of the antibiotics. If nothing else, he needed to make the best of the situation and *not* be a pain in the neck for Darius and, by extension, Captain Brady. That was the important thing, he reminded himself.

As the food and beer arrived, he looked questioningly at Colin.

The bartender shook his head. "Nothing funky in it, relax and enjoy it. Our cook is actually pretty good, that's why we're so busy at lunch."

Jeff grinned at him. "Thanks." As he took his first bite, he realized that the statement was correct—this was one of the best burgers he'd had in quite a while. He followed it with a sip of beer and settled in to wait for things to start happening, which would probably be around midnight. *It's going to be a long night.*

CHAPTER 34

Later that night, Darius showed up again back at the Pigeonhole. "Tonight we're hitting a gun shop. It's about three miles away and I'll need all of you to get the stuff out of there in a hurry. We'll take four cars … if anything goes wrong, scatter. We'll meet back here afterwards. Any questions?"

"Darius," Jeff said, "won't they have an alarm system?"

"Yeah, they do, but I have the code for it. As soon as you bust down the door, I'll enter the code. That should give us some extra time. Anything else?"

"One more," Jeff said, "do they leave the guns out all night or do they lock them up in a safe?"

Darius grinned at him. "You're starting to think like I do. They leave them out in the cases; we've checked it out already."

With that, the group of them headed out, Darius in the lead car. Jeff climbed in the car that Willum was driving, along with two other guys he'd seen before, but hadn't met. There was no small talk, this was all business.

Martin's Guns was in an out-of-the-way place, surrounded by auto repair shops, a laundromat, and some kind of food products place. *That's probably why he picked this one*, Jeff thought. The cars went around the building to the back so they weren't obvious to passers-by, and everyone got out, leaving the motors running. Jeff noticed that there wasn't a second floor, so there was no likelihood of anyone living on the premises like a few weeks ago when two of them were shot.

Darius led them to the back door. "This is the door they normally use to go in and out, mornings and evenings. Jeff, blow out the door, nothing more."

Leaning back against one of the cars, Jeff focused on the door and attempted to blow it. It proved harder than he expected, so he tried again and, with a wrenching squeal, it crashed into the hallway inside the shop.

Darius ran inside and punched in the code to stop the alarm from going off. Apparently there was a short delay so the owner could disable the system when he went in. There were no alarms that they heard. With that done, Darius waved the rest of the men into the shop, each of them carrying a canvas bag to throw guns in. Most of them smashed the cases and pulled out the pistols, while a few of them went for the rifles and shotguns on the wall.

"Jeff, come here. Quick!" Darius yelled.

As he went in, he immediately saw that while the pistols were lying loose in the cases, the rifles had a cable through the trigger guards, to lock them in place. Before Darius could even say anything, Jeff thought about the locks and destroyed them, freeing the cable from both ends, so they could pull the weapons down and toss them in the bags.

The whole operation took less than five minutes. The guns were loaded into the trunks and back seats of the cars and they were gone, driving back to the Pigeonhole separate ways so as not to arouse suspicion in case anyone saw them.

In the lot behind the bar, they loaded the guns into two of the cars, with room for only the drivers, and they drove off. Jeff wondered where they were going, but wasn't about to ask. It did make sense to him to not have them near the bar where they always met.

As they watched the two cars turn the corner, Darius said, "Good job, guys. Drinks are on the house, like usual."

CHAPTER 35

The next morning, Jeff woke late. As he walked into the kitchen and smelled the aroma of bacon, and said, "Thanks for making breakfast, Mom."

Beatriz gave him an odd look before turning back to the eggs. "Is your shoulder still bleeding like last week?"

Jeff shook his head. "No, it's healing nicely now that I got the antibiotics."

"Can I see if it's healing okay?"

"Don't worry about it. It's fine."

She shook her head. "It's a gunshot wound, isn't it?"

Jeff looked over at her. "Why would you even think that?"

"If it was anything else, you would have gone to a doctor, but you didn't. Anya told me that much."

Jeff didn't answer right away, then changed tactics. "I'm going to get her out of the shower before breakfast gets cold."

To his back, Beatriz said, "I'm not stupid."

A couple of minutes later he returned with Anya, who had been dressing anyway. As they walked in the room, Jeff said, "Yeah, Mom, I know you're not stupid. I'm trying to keep other people out of this as much as possible so they don't get hurt."

"You mean like my broken arm? I should use this cast to knock some sense into you."

Anya laughed. "Hey, that's a good idea!"

Jeff frowned at both of them and helped himself to some bacon, eggs, and juice, fumbling since he was forced to use one hand. Maybe ignoring them would work.

A little later Jeff asked Beatriz, "So do you have all your furniture and stuff settled now?"

"No," Beatriz replied, "I'm still not sure where to go with the rest of the furniture. The living room filled up quickly, but there's still more in the garage. Any suggestions?"

"Well, there's room in the attic but you can't get to it easily. We could put some in the fourth bedroom if you want, so you have access to it. What do you think?"

"Let me think about it for a few days. It's okay in the garage for now."

Jeff nodded and started to walk away, but Beatriz stopped him and put her arms around him. "Don't get shot again, okay?"

He laughed. "Sure, Mom, avoiding that is pretty high on my list."

"Always the joker, huh?"

CHAPTER 36

A few days later, the front door opened as they sat down to dinner and Laura came in, eyes red, looking tired and angry.

"Marcus didn't hurt you, did he?"

"Of course not. If he tried, I'd slug him."

"Want some dinner then?" Jeff asked, eyebrows raised.

She shook her head. "No, I want to talk to you."

"Can we talk during dinner? I'm pretty hungry."

"No, I'll wait."

"You need a drink or something? We have vodka. I could make you a Moscow mule…"

'No, go ahead and eat." With that, she plopped down on the couch and frowned.

Jeff pursed his lips for a moment. "Is something wrong with you and Marcus?"

"As if."

"Look, Laura, if you want to talk to me there is nothing here that Anya or Mom Onofre can't hear."

Taking her time, she got up off the couch and sat down at the table, grabbing a chicken leg and biting into it.

"You want a plate?" Jeff asked.

"Stop it. If I want something, I'll get it."

Jeff took another bite of food and rolled his eyes at Anya and Beatriz questioningly. Anya shrugged. There was no response from Beatriz.

After a couple of minutes, Laura dropped the remains of her chicken leg on Jeff's plate, went to the sink and washed her hands. "Okay, what is going on with you? You won't talk to Marcus—you pretend there is no problem at all. You haven't told me anything though your shoulder is bleeding and you're wearing that sling. Mom doesn't know what's going on either, and we're both worried."

Jeff put down his fork and took a sip of wine. "Fine, what do you want to know? But, before you ask, I'm not going to tell you any details that could put you in danger—or Mom, or Marcus."

Laura frowned at this as she thought about it. "Okay, let's start with the basics. What happened to your shoulder? Why were you playing rugby?"

Jeff pursed his lips. "Do not, under any

circumstances, tell Marcus what I'm about to tell you. Agreed?"

"Why not?" she countered.

"Because once Marcus gets something in his head, there is no stopping him. He keeps going without thinking through the consequences. In this case, that could get him killed. Maybe you too. Literally."

Laura stared at him for a moment. "Literally?"

Jeff nodded.

Laura shook her head. "This is weird—okay, I won't tell him unless you tell me it's okay to."

Jeff took another sip of wine. "You're right, it's not from rugby. It's a gunshot."

Laura leaped up, bumping the table and knocking over two of the wine glasses. "What? A gunshot? What are you into, you idiot?"

As Beatriz got up to clean up the mess, Anya said, "Laura, sit down. We'll explain it. It's my fault."

"No, it is not!" Jeff responded. "We're both victims here, so don't tell her that."

Laura looked from one to the other, then over at Beatriz. "You know about this, too?"

Beatriz nodded. "I figured out what they didn't tell me. They didn't want to worry me. Instead, I got a broken arm. It makes no sense. It is not their fault."

Laura blinked several times, as she slowly sat down. She picked up Jeff's wine glass, the only one that hadn't been knocked over, and drank half of what was left. Looking at her brother, she asked, "You're not going to pick me up again, are you?"

Jeff chuckled. "Only if you get out of control again like you just did. Do you want to hear details, or not?"

She picked up Jeff's glass again and drank the rest of the wine. "Fine, talk."

Anya started out at the beginning, when they first met Willum in the alley, and followed it through to the trip to Carson City, and to where things were now, leaving out most of the details.

As she seemed to be wrapping up, Laura said, "Wait. Before you said it was your fault, what did you mean?"

"It isn't her fault at all," said Jeff.

Anya shook her head. "I'm the hostage. If he doesn't play along, they've threatened to gang-rape me."

Still sitting in the chair, Laura gaped at her, turning pale. "Oh, my God!"

Before she could say anything else, Jeff asked, "Now do you see why I don't want you or Mom or Marcus involved in this? These are *not* nice people. But as long as I give them what they want, we're okay."

"What exactly do you have to give them?"

"Brute force. I knock out windows, flip cars over, break down doors. We broke into a small shop and the owner lived upstairs. He shot me and another guy."

Laura watched him. "What did the doctors say?"

Jeff took a deep breath, shaking his head, then said, "Laura, you don't go to the doctor with a gunshot wound when you're involved in breaking and entering. If I did that I'd be in jail."

"But you'd be safe, at least for a while."

Jeff shook his head. "And what about Anya?"

She sat there, stunned. "Oh, shit."

After a few minutes, Laura continued. "Jeff, there must be someone we can turn to for help."

"Stop right there," he said. "This is not a 'we' situation. You and Marcus and Mom need to stay as far away from this as possible. Otherwise it's even riskier for me because I don't know everything that's going on and there's more chance of a leak somewhere.

"And yes, there is someone to turn to, but it has its own risk. Police corruption is handled by the FBI, so I could talk to them about the captain involved and the whole gang. They would investigate. And if it came out during the investigation that I'm a freak who can do this stuff, which it would, what happens then? They lock me up so they can study me? I disappear in the interest of public protection?

"I've thought about it from all angles. There are two problems here. I don't know how far up this goes in the police department. I only know of one person, but others could be involved, maybe payoffs. I know it sounds paranoid, but that's where I am right now. One word or even suspicion from the wrong person and I'm dead, and Anya's at risk."

Laura shook her head. "They wouldn't do that to her if you were dead. There's no point to it."

"Look, Laura, I've been there when they've had women in the back room that they kidnapped. I heard the screams, and moans. And the next day there was a body found floating in the river with bruises on the wrists and ankles where she was tied down. You're way over your head here. So am I, but don't make it worse for me.

"For now at least, I'm playing along until I can figure something else out. Can you forget you heard about it? Or are you going to make trouble for me, too?"

Laura was turning pale again. "I can't very well forget about it. I'll probably have nightmares knowing this." She paused for a long time. "Okay, I'll stay out of it. I'm worried about you. But I won't tell anyone else, not even Mom."

Jeff nodded, and got up to grab another bottle of wine.

CHAPTER 37

The following weekend, Jeff and Anya were in the car. "Jeff, where are we going? We've been driving for an hour already," Anya asked.

"Relax. We'll be there in about ten minutes."

"Where is there? And why are you driving so slowly? You never pay attention to speed limits," Anya commented.

"Think of it as the new me."

Anya shook her head, tapping her fingers on the armrest.

Jeff sighed. "Okay, here's the deal. We're going to check on my uncle's farm. It's out here in the middle of nowhere."

"Is something wrong with him?"

"No, he's out of town this week and wanted someone to check up on it."

"So I don't get to meet him?"

"Nope. He lives alone out here, in spite of Mom's request that he move into the city. He seems to love the peace and quiet and I can't say I blame him. We used to come out here when we were kids and run around all over the place. It was loads of fun, and Laura and I would fall asleep on the way home while Dad was driving."

"Oh, so we're only going to be here a few minutes?"

"No," he replied, "I thought we'd hang around for a while and wander about. I even brought us lunch."

Anya scowled. "And what's in the other bag in the trunk that you were trying to hide?"

As he turned into a gravel driveway, he said, "Oh, that's a pistol. I want to practice with it."

Anya twisted a lock of hair around her finger. "I haven't heard about this before. When did you get that?"

"Last week," he responded, keeping a straight face.

Anya turned in her seat and looked at him. "Is this from Darius?"

Caught, he frowned and said, "Yeah, he wants me to have it and learn how to use it. Not that I'll need it. It's not in my job description."

"Very funny. Is that why you're driving the speed limit, too?"

"Well, I wouldn't want to get stopped while it's in the trunk."

"Let me guess—it's not registered?"

"Can't be. All the serial numbers have been ground off so it's harder to trace."

Anya was quiet for a minute, staring out the windshield. "Jeff, I don't like this at all."

"I know. I agree entirely, but there's not much choice here. In fact, I want you to practice with it, too."

Her head snapped around to look at him. "What?"

He stopped the car in front of a metal gate and got out to open it, then climbed back in.

"Jeff, I don't want to do this."

"Anya, your mother has a gun. Have you ever fired it?"

A pout appeared. "A few times, and I didn't like it."

"And why did she want you to do that?"

Frowning more, "She said I needed to know how."

"And that's all I want. I want you to know how to handle it for your own protection."

"And you waited until we got here to spring this on me?"

"Well, I kind of thought you might not be real agreeable about this idea."

"Great, now I have to watch out for you, too. What happened to telling me the truth all the time?"

"Anya, please. I want you safe, but I can't always be there with you. You know that. And I do not trust these people I'm dealing with. Play along for a while, please?"

She turned to look across the farm while he got out to close the gate behind them.

"Are you going to pout now?"

"Yes. Leave me alone."

As he stopped the car in front of the large log home, Jeff said, "Do you want me to roll down the windows for you or would you rather steam up the inside of the car yourself?"

"Stop trying to be funny." She opened the door and got out, heading up onto the porch next to him. "This seems like a nice place."

He grabbed a key from the top of the door frame and let them in. The living room had a large fireplace and a number of early American chairs and sofa. The wood floor shone like it had been polished. The kitchen, right behind the living room, was contemporary with a ceramic tile floor and granite countertops.

"Wow, does he live here by himself? It's neat as a pin."

"Yeah. Uncle Louie is a neat freak. I apparently didn't get that gene."

They wandered through the house, checking each of the bedrooms and making sure the windows were locked and secure. "Looks like everything is okay in here. Let's go out back."

As they walked out onto the porch, Anya noticed a small pond down the hill, near the bottom of a grassy field that bordered on a wooded area. "That looks nice. How come the water is so blue?"

"No livestock around here and it's only stocked with bluegill and bass. No bottom feeders to muddy it up. Besides that, the bottom is mostly sand."

"Did you bring our swimsuits, too?"

Jeff pointedly looked around. The house blocked the road and there was not another building in sight. "Think we need them?"

She followed his gaze and grinned. "This could be fun."

"First things first. Let's wander down to the creek and practice for a while, then we can take a swim."

Anya frowned, but didn't argue.

About a half-hour later, they made their way back up

the hill from the creek where they were shooting. Jeff was surprised that Anya handled the gun well, and managed to hit some of the tin cans they had dug out of his uncle's trash. Dropping the gun off in the trunk of the car, Jeff grabbed the lunch cooler and a beach towel. They headed down to the pond and spread out the towel on a sandy spot.

"Can't swim after we eat," commented Anya.

"Works for me." He grinned as they took off their clothes. When Anya slipped out of her underwear, he commented, "Our baby's getting big. And you look even more beautiful than ever."

She blushed before wading into the shallows, then dove head first into the deeper end. Coming back up and treading water, she said "Don't you think I look like a whale?"

He grinned. "Not a bit, sweetheart."

CHAPTER 38

Several weeks later, on another normal Friday night, Jeff walked into the Pigeonhole and was surprised that Darius immediately walked over to greet him.

"Hey, did you get a chance to practice with that pistol yet?"

"Sure did. Ran a couple of boxes of ammo through it. Doesn't have as much kick as I was expecting."

"Okay, good. Well, I have a job for tonight. Shouldn't take long, but I need you with us."

"I'm ready when you are."

"Let's give it a couple of hours before we go so things quiet down in the neighborhood."

Jeff nodded and got a beer.

Three hours later, Darius rounded up a couple of guys to go with them and they drove over to the north side of town in a beat-up car they used when they were trying to be inconspicuous. This district was slowly going derelict, with abandoned buildings on both sides of the street, including some with missing walls that looked like they could collapse any minute.

When Jeff looked around, wondering what they were doing here, he saw only one person moving on the street.

The driver pulled the car around to the back lot of an abandoned bank building and stopped behind some bushes and overgrown weeds. The four of them got out.

"This place is abandoned. What are we doing here?" Jeff asked.

Darius looked at Jeff and handed him a flashlight. "You still ask too many questions. You'll see in a minute." Pointing to the back door, formerly an employees' entrance, he said, "Open the door."

The door was old and in poor shape. Jeff obliged by blowing it into the building, ripping it out of its frame without making a huge racket.

Darius pointed to the two guys with them and said, "Cover the front and back. Let me know immediately if you see anything odd." Brandishing his flashlight, he turned to Jeff, "There's no power to the building, so we'll probably need these, but be careful with them because someone might drive by and see us through the front window."

Jeff nodded as he followed his boss into the building. He was puzzled; there wasn't anything of value in here and he didn't see the point.

Darius clicked on his flashlight and led the way in. All

of the internal doors were open and the floor and counters were covered with a coating of dust that drifted into the air as they walked through. Leading them to the front lobby, Darius turned left and went into a small anteroom in front of the open vault. "Okay, perfect. Help me seal this vault up."

Even though it hadn't been moved in years, the vault door swung closed easily and Darius spun the handle on the front to lock it in place. "Okay, dude, now it's your turn. I want you to blow the vault door."

Jeff shook his head. "Umm, okay, but can you tell me why?"

Darius frowned at him again. "You and your damn questions. I need to make sure you can do this before we go live."

Jeff's eyes opened wider and his voice went up a notch. "We're going to rob a bank?"

"Shut up and do it."

Jeff backed up to brace himself against the wall and stared at the door for a moment. He stuck the flashlight in his back pocket. Focusing his attention on the door, he pushed with his mind. It wobbled, but didn't open.

He was about to say he couldn't do it when he thought of Anya. It always came down to her; he couldn't say no. Getting angry, he briefly thought about slamming Darius into the wall, but that left too many loose ends, and he knew what the result would be. Instead, he channeled his anger and focused again on the door. There was a creaking noise and the plaster wall on either side crumbled a little.

Anya, I have to think of Anya. His head felt like it was about to burst, but he ignored the pain. Summoning all his mental strength, he slammed the door, which made a huge racket when it crashed back into the vault, still partially hanging from one hinge, leaving the air filled with dust when the final pieces fell to the floor. He slumped to his knees, unable to move.

"Let's get out of here." Darius said as he trotted across the room and grabbed Jeff by the arms, dragging him to his feet, and pulling him out of the room.

"I got this," Jeff mumbled, wrenching free of Darius, who continued ahead, with Jeff stumbling out of the building after him, trying to keep up.

As they reached the car, Darius opened the door and shoved him into the back seat, then gave a brief, sharp whistle to summon the others. Within minutes they were down the block and out of sight.

CHAPTER 39

Half an hour later, even after another beer and a couple of ibuprofens, Jeff could barely stand up. He sat in a booth in the back of the room, ignoring everything going on around him. His eyes had trouble trying to focus with his massive headache.

"Hey, dude, you need something for the pain?" asked Darius.

"What did you have in mind?"

"I've got some pills here that will fix you up fine."

"What are they?" mumbled Jeff.

"You know, pain-killers. The same stuff everybody uses."

Jeff thought about it for a moment, and shook his head. "Yeah, no thanks. The headache will go away in a little while."

"Well, you need a ride home? Willum can take you, if you want. We can even get somebody to take your car."

Jeff shook his head again. As far as he knew, they

didn't know where he was living now and he wasn't about to help them find out. "Thanks, but I'll be okay. Are you done with me tonight?"

"Yep," Darius responded. "You did a great job breaking through that vault door. I wasn't sure you could do it."

"Yeah, neither was I."

Darius wandered off and Jeff took another sip of beer, then pulled out his cell phone. "Marcus, can you help me? I need a ride."

"Yeah, sure. What's up?"

"I need a ride home. I've had too much to drink and shouldn't be driving."

"Okay, where are you?"

Jeff gave him the address of the pharmacist down the street, far enough away that Marcus wouldn't know where he'd been and no one from the gang would see him.

"I'll be there in about ten minutes, okay?"

"Yeah, thanks, bro."

Leaving the rest of his beer on the table, Jeff wandered out the front door like he was going out for some fresh air. When he thought no one would see him, he staggered down the street to the pharmacist's shop, which was closed at this time of night.

About fifteen minutes later he saw Marcus's car creeping up the street, so he flagged him down.

"Wow, you must be totally wasted. I've never seen you like this before," Marcus commented as Jeff eased himself into the passenger seat.

"Yeah. Just go. Take a left at the next street."

Marcus frowned. "You know, I still remember how to drive."

Jeff nodded, close to passing out, and mumbled, "Okay, drive."

After about five minutes, Marcus asked, "How come you're out drinking without your wife? And in this part of town?"

Jeff, still barely functional, looked over at Marcus and said, "Can we drop it? I don't answer to you, and I'm sure I'll hear about it when I get home."

Marcus shook his head. "Yeah, fine. Whatever you want."

A few minutes later, as they pulled up in front of Jeff's house, he said, "Look, Marcus, thanks for coming for me at short notice. I appreciate it. Do not, under any circumstances, tell anyone where you picked me up. Got that?"

Marcus studied him for a moment. "Dude, what are you into?"

Jeff looked him in the eye and said, "Stuff that could get you killed."

Marcus stared at his friend as he got out of the car and shuffled up to the front door.

CHAPTER 40

Anya's mother opened the door as he approached, saving him the trouble of finding his keys.

Looking him over, and watching the way he crept into the room, she said, "What did they do to you?"

As he slumped onto the couch, he said, "Nothing. I did it all to myself."

"Okay, then, what hurts?"

"My head. Everything else is okay. Where is Anya?"

"She got into the shower, should be out in a few minutes." She paused for a moment, "Unless you decide to join her."

Jeff chuckled. Beatriz understood them both very well, not that it surprised him. But her openness sometimes caught him off guard. "Not tonight, I've got a headache."

Beatriz laughed and said, "If you need anything, let me know."

"Thanks, Mom."

He pulled himself up off the couch, stumbled to the stairs and made his way to their bedroom. The shower was still running so he flopped on his back on the bed, closing his eyes.

In a few minutes, Anya came out of the bathroom wrapped in a towel and jumped when she saw him on the bed. "Oh, you're home a lot earlier than usual. Is it a special occasion?"

"Yes. I feel like I've died."

"Jeff, that is not funny."

"They were done with me for the evening and I called Marcus to come drive me home."

Frowning, she asked, "Why did you call Marcus? Is something wrong with the car?"

He shook his head. "No, it's fine. I have a massive headache and didn't trust myself to drive."

"Couldn't one of the guys drive you home?"

He looked at her, appraising. "Not sure they know where we live, and I'm not going to make it easy for them."

She straightened up, startled. "Oh, I wasn't thinking. I'm glad you were. What can I do for your head? Want me to rub your temples? Get an ice pack?"

"The temples thing might help."

She climbed up on the bed and straddled his hips, then leaned forward and started massaging his temples.

As he relaxed into the gentle sensation, the towel came untucked and fell open. "Hmm," he said, "This sure got interesting very quickly."

Anya smirked at him and threw the towel on the floor. "Anything else you want?"

"Well, this wasn't in my plan, but I think maybe there is."

She smiled down at him. "Anything you want…"

***

A little while later they were lying in bed, cuddling.

"So, what gave you the headache tonight?"

Jeff shrugged and mumbled, "I had to blow a bank vault."

Anya sat up, instantly alert. "You robbed a bank?"

"Yes, a closed one with nothing in it."

She frowned and her shoulders relaxed a bit. "Why would you do that?"

Jeff didn't want to continue this conversation, but he figured he owed it to her. "Apparently, Darius is making plans to do a real bank and wanted to be sure

I could blow the vault."

Anya sat still for a few moments, then said, "Jeff, you know I don't like this."

"Yeah. And you know I don't have a choice."

CHAPTER 41

"What, exactly, is your brother up to?" Marcus asked.

Laura looked over at him, caution showing in her eyes. "Why do you ask?"

"Well, you know he asked me to pick him up last night. Said he was too drunk to drive, but he looked totally miserable and he was grumpy as hell. Plus, he was in a bad part of town, and without Anya. It seems so wrong. Then, when I asked what he was up to, he said it could get me killed. The way he looked at me, I believed him."

Laura sighed, wondering what to tell him that was believable. "Look, he owes some favors to some bad people because of a stupid mistake he made a while back. The stress from it is giving him migraines, which I can understand. That's probably what happened last night."

Marcus looked at her, doubting. "What kind of trouble?"

"I don't know. He wouldn't tell me either, just told me to stay out of it."

"Well, I'd really like to help him out if there is something I can do."

Laura jumped to her feet. "NO!"

Eyes wide, Marcus backed up and stared at her.

"Marcus, leave it alone. I swear to God, if you try to do anything, if you even try to talk to him about it, I will walk out of this apartment and you will never see me again."

"Laura, relax a little bit—I've never seen you get this upset about anything."

"Of course I'm upset! You have no idea what you're messing with, and I suspect Jeff was right. If you mess with this it could get both of you killed."

Frowning, he asked, "So you know what he's doing?"

She sighed, trying to get hold of her temper. "To some extent. I don't know all the details and don't want to. It's risky even knowing."

"Well, can't he go to the police? Or leave town? Or something?"

She pressed her lips together for a moment. "Why do you think they went to Nevada to get married and didn't tell anyone about it in advance?"

A light clicked on. "That was what the wedding was about?"

"No, not the wedding. They wanted to get married, but they were hoping they could get away and get lost somewhere nobody could find them. It didn't work out that way at all."

"Isn't there something we can do?"

Laura frowned at him again. "And risk getting my brother killed?"

"Well, no. There must be another way."

She closed her eyes for a moment. "Marcus, it's not our choice to make. It's Jeff's. He insisted that anything you or I could do would make it worse for him and I believe him. Please, you have to drop it."

"What about Anya? Is she involved too?"

Recalling what her brother had told her about the threats, she shook her head. "No. She knows what he is doing and believes it's the best thing, but she doesn't like it either, not at all."

"Is there something we can do to help her?"

"Marcus, stop right there. If you say one more word about this, I'm walking out the door now and really will *never* see you again. And that includes talking to Anya, Beatriz, my Mom, or anyone else. Do you understand?"

He started to say something then stopped, mouth open. Staring at her for a long moment, he finally said, "What do you want for dinner?"

CHAPTER 42

"Where is Anya?"

Beatriz looked up from mixing something in a bowl and said, "She went to the grocery store to pick up some things. I guess you slept in?"

"Yeah, didn't even notice her getting out of bed this morning. How long ago was it?"

"A little over an hour. She had breakfast with me before she left. When I heard you moving around upstairs, I figured you would probably be hungry."

"Thanks. I am."

Beatriz poured some batter into the frying pan. "Pancakes are okay, right?"

"Yeah, sure. I could eat a horse."

"Okay, I'll go shopping for one later."

Jeff grinned at her, saying nothing as she flipped the pancakes and poured him some coffee.

After he had finished eating, he got up from the table to leave the room.

"Can we talk for a minute?"

Jeff nodded. "Sure, about what?"

"Sit back down."

Beatriz was not normally vague, so he sat down, puzzled, as she sat across from him.

"You're right-handed, correct?"

"Yeah…"

"Give me your right hand."

"Are you doing a palm reading?"

"Yes, for my own benefit. It's what I do. Humor me."

Jeff thought about asking if she needed her robes, but thought better of it. He stuck out his hand and she took it in hers, examining it in great detail. This went on for about ten minutes with nothing from Beatriz except some hmms and an occasional mumbled phrase that he couldn't quite hear.

After five more minutes, she let go of his hand and looked up, watching him. "Okay, thanks."

"Well, are you going to tell me?"

"No, this was for me. I told you that."

Jeff shook his head. "That's not fair, it's my reading."

"And sometimes you're better off not knowing."

"Is it that bad?"

"I didn't say it was bad, but it looks like things are going to be pretty difficult for you for a while."

"Anything specific I should know about?"

"No, it shows more of the same stuff going on, probably with the gang, though it looks like there might be a change for the better in your real job. I don't know the specifics, though."

When she didn't elaborate, he asked, "Is that all you're going to tell me?"

"It was one of the murkiest readings I've ever seen. That doesn't mean it's bad, just your future is not clear. Anya and the baby are in there and everything seemed fine from that perspective. It's the gang stuff that's messing it up." She shrugged as Anya walked in the door carrying bags of groceries.

CHAPTER 43

On Monday morning, before Jeff was up, Beatriz said, "Let's talk for a few minutes."

Walking away, Anya looked back over her shoulder at her mother. "Yeah, sure. About what?"

"I wanted to tell you about Jeff's reading."

"Wait. He let you do a reading? He would never let me do one!"

"I think with this Mom thing going on, he doesn't want to upset me, so he let me. Come to think of it, I didn't exactly ask him, I told him I was going to do it."

"Well, that's not fair. I *am* his wife, after all."

"Anya, we've had this discussion before. If you want fair, go roll some dice. If you're talking about people, forget it."

Anya pressed her lips together, scowling at her mother.

"I did the reading on Saturday when you were out getting groceries. Since you weren't here, it seemed like a good time. I thought he might prefer the privacy."

"And you waited until Monday to tell me?" she asked, looking annoyed.

"Anya, cool down. Yes, I waited until you and I were alone. You two are always together unless Jeff is gone to one of his two jobs."

Anya shook her head, resigned. "Fine, tell me about it."

As Anya sat down at the kitchen table, Beatriz asked, "By the way, how is Baby Merriwether doing these days? You're not saying much."

"The baby keeps kicking me, especially in the middle of the night. Makes it hard to sleep. And we're not calling it Baby Merriwether anymore, we're calling it Lumpy because that's how it feels."

Beatriz stifled a laugh as she pulled up a chair and sat across from her daughter. "Hmm, I see."

Looking up, Anya asked, "Okay, so what about the reading?"

"Do you remember the blackness you saw when you read Lainie's palm? The one you asked me about?"

"Sure, what about it?"

Putting her hands across the table on top of Anya's, Beatriz said, "I saw the same thing in Jeff's."

"Oh my God, you didn't tell him, did you?"

"Don't be ridiculous. You know I wouldn't do that."

"Well, what else did you see?"

"Looks like," she paused for a moment, "*Lumpy* will be fine. And from Jeff's point of view, your relationship will be fine. He loves you a lot, you know."

Anya grinned, "Well, at least that's good to hear. Any idea what the black part is?"

"No," she mumbled. "You never can tell with something like that. Could be something terrible, or it could be something simple, like a misunderstanding." She shrugged. "It does look like he might get a promotion in the near future."

Anya looked shocked. "In the gang?"

"Of course not, in his real job. Gangs don't give promotions."

"Well, that would surprise me, since it always seems like he's under a lot of stress. I tell him to relax but he doesn't seem to know how." She paused. "Well, except when we make love."

"Anya, put yourself in his place. He's under a great deal of pressure and always looking over his shoulder."

The younger woman shook her head. "Yeah, I guess

you're right. I should be nicer to him than I am. Maybe even to you, too. The other day I was thinking about putting you in an old folks' home."

Beatriz laughed. "I'm only forty-two, so I don't think you'll get away with that." She paused for a long time. "You know, thinking back, I was real grumpy and had a bunch of weird ideas right before you were born. I guess it runs in the family."

CHAPTER 44

The usual gang members were gathered at the Pigeonhole on Friday night. Jeff looked around, saw no one he wanted to talk to, then went to the bar to get a beer. After chatting with Colin for a couple of minutes, he wandered over to a booth in the corner and sat by himself.

A couple of minutes later, Willum passed by, nodding to him, saying nothing.

Jeff was hoping this was going to be one of the nights when they did nothing. On those rare occasions, he usually got out earlier and went home since he had no interest in hanging out with the gang. Just as he was starting to think it was a real possibility, Darius came out of the back room, looked around, then came over to sit across from him.

"Jeff, we're going to need you in a couple of hours, so don't go anywhere."

"Umm, okay. Is this about the thing we did the practice run for?"

Darius shook his head and frowned. "Always questions. Nope, that one is still a ways off. Tonight should be pretty quick and simple. You'll see,"

Knowing he wouldn't get any more information, Jeff took a sip of his beer, saying nothing as Darius got up and wandered off.

A few minutes later, Willum came back with a beer and sat down across from him. "Looks like I'm driving again tonight. It's a small group, so only one car. We're taking the old Blazer that I've been in lately."

"Any idea where were going?" Jeff asked.

Willum shook his head. "Nah, we never find out until we get there. You should know that by now. Anyways, all you have to do is come along for the ride, do one minute of the hard work and then you're done. Well, until we split the profits. You should get used to it."

Jeff nodded. "Well, yeah. I can hope, though."

Willum laughed at that, then left to talk to a couple of guys that had come in.

About three hours and two beers later, Darius rounded up the group and got them into the Blazer, not explaining anything.

Jeff looked around, then quipped, "Are we going four-wheeling tonight?"

Darius grimaced and shook his head. A couple of the other guys chuckled.

They drove into a nicer part of town along a main drive that still carried a lot of traffic, even at one in the morning, but that didn't seem to bother Darius. Willum turned into a strip mall and drove the length of it. The only interesting things Jeff saw were a bar at one end that was still crowded and a jewelry store near the middle, four shops down from the bar.

Willum went to the far end then took the SUV around the back and pulled up behind the jewelry shop, partially hidden behind some large trash dumpsters. He turned off the lights but left the engine running.

Darius turned to them. "Okay, here's the deal. Jeff, you blow the back door, then I'll turn off the security system while you go blow the safe which is somewhere in the back room. Lawrence, you and the other two empty the safe into your bags, then we're out of here. Willum is staying in the car so we don't have any delays."

As they got out, Jeff noticed that the interior car lights didn't come on the way they normally would. Security precaution, he presumed.

Leaning back against the vehicle, Jeff blew the back door into the shop. Darius ran inside to get the alarm, Jeff and the others right behind him.

It was easy to spot the safe: five feet high, feet bolted to the concrete floor. Lawrence lit it up with his flashlight while Jeff leaned back against a wall and, after two tries, broke through the door. The other guys grabbed their bags and loaded up the jewelry while Jeff went back out and got in the car. Two minutes later, the other guys came out and jumped in and Willum hit the gas.

There was a shout as they pulled away, but Willum accelerated. Then a bullet shattered the rear window, missing all of them but covering them with shards. Everyone but Willum crouched down when more shots were fired. A side window shattered as they turned the corner, and Willum slid the Blazer out into the street and mashed the gas pedal to the floor. Two blocks later, they turned off on a side street and Willum killed the headlights, but kept going. After several more turns, they were back at the Pigeonhole. Everyone piled out in the back lot, while Willum took the SUV and dumped it in a different part of town.

Darius was in a good mood after they stashed the jewelry and came back into the bar. He ordered beers for everyone then came over to talk to Jeff. "You did good again tonight. That hit should give us a nice load of cash once I get rid of the stuff. I really love these places that are too stupid to reset the factory passwords on their alarm systems. It's like they're asking to get robbed."

Jeff nodded. "Yeah, the gunshots were a surprise."

"Comes with the territory. I'm guessing the bartender was taking out trash and had his piece with him. An unlucky coincidence. By the way, we're done for tonight, so if you want to split, go ahead."

Jeff nodded, downed his beer, and headed for his car.

CHAPTER 45

On Wednesday, Jeff was sitting at his desk when his boss Dan came over.

"Hey, Dan, what's up?"

"Well, Steven wants to talk to you when you get a couple of minutes,' he said with a grin.

Jeff shook his head. The last time he had talked to Dan's boss Steven was about a year ago, when he had done something stupid and was being called on it. "Am I in trouble again?"

Dan smiled again. "Only one way to find out." He nodded towards Steven's office.

Jeff shuffled papers on his desk for a few minutes, then got up and went to talk to Steven.

"Jeff, close the door and pull up a chair."

Jeff did so, then wiped his sweaty palms on his pants, thinking this was going to get worse, but he said nothing. Though, thinking back, he couldn't remember anything he'd done wrong in the recent past.

"Jeff, I was talking to Dan the other day and he pointed out that you are doing really well lately. Says you've been spending a lot of Friday nights in here to get your stuff cleaned up. Is that an accurate statement?"

Confused, Jeff nodded, and said, "Well, I have been in here a lot on Friday evenings."

"Having trouble keeping up with the work?"

"No, I want to stay on top of things. One step ahead of the game."

Steven nodded. "That's exactly what Dan thought, and it makes sense to me. That's the mark of the kind of people we need around here, and that kind of dedication to the company is appreciated."

Wondering where this was going, Jeff nodded. "Thanks, I'm glad to hear that."

"So, I wanted to ask you if you're ready to take on Dan's job."

Jeff snapped his head back, looking dazed. "What? Is Dan going somewhere?"

Steven laughed. "Well, we have a new position open in the Claims Department, and Dan is the ideal person to fill that. So, he is planning on moving up as soon as we find someone to take his job. And I'm thinking that you're the right person, but I wanted to talk to you first."

Jeff stared at him for a moment. "Thank you, Steven. I'm pleased to be considered for this. It wasn't something I expected."

Steven nodded. "Sometimes the best things happen that way. You seem a little surprised, and I understand that. Do you have any questions for me?"

"Not … not right now," Jeff stammered.

"Obviously, this promotion would come with a nice raise, as I'm sure you guessed. Since you seem surprised, why don't you think about it for a day or two and then give me your answer?"

"Okay, I'll do that." Jeff paused. "Though I don't think it will take a lot of thought."

Steven gave a wide grin. "You know, that's exactly what I expected from you. Let me know when you're ready."

Jeff nodded, stood up and shook his hand. "Thanks again."

***

That evening Jeff and Anya were lying in bed, discussing the offer that Jeff's boss had made to him.

"It would be a good position, a stepping stone on the corporate ladder, and I don't see any reason not to take it."

Anya sighed. "The odd thing about it is that it's

partially because of the stuff you're doing with the gang. If it wasn't for that, you wouldn't be in there all those Friday nights."

Jeff nodded, "Well, that is true. It's kind of having a round-about good effect on things."

Anya looked over at him, pausing and biting her lip, then put her head in her hands, sobbing.

Jeff slipped his arm around her and pulled her close. "Anya, what's wrong? I thought this was a good thing. Why are you crying?"

She sobbed a few more times, then caught her breath. "It is. I'm happy for you … for us."

Jeff frowned, watching her eyes. "Is this one of these 'I'm crying because I'm happy' things?"

Anya let out another sob, then shook her head. "No. It's good that this is happening." She paused again, wiping away some of the tears. "It's that I want us to have a normal life for a change where something like this is a cause to celebrate without being overshadowed by the gang threat that's over our head. I'm scared."

Putting his other arm around her, too, Jeff kissed her forehead and then lifted her chin to look into her eyes. "I know what you mean. I wish I had an answer."

Anya leaned into him, putting her head on his chest,

still crying.

Jeff sat there, comforting her, and wondering to himself how he was going to resolve this.

CHAPTER 46

The following Friday, the day after Jeff accepted the offer of Dan's job, Jeff was in the Pigeonhole as usual. It was quiet again, with nothing going on in the back room, based on what he was *not* hearing, but that was part of the activities Jeff never had anything to do with, and didn't want any more details.

After a couple of hours, Darius and Willum wandered over and sat down across from Jeff. "So, here's the deal," Darius said. "We've got another job tonight, but we don't do anything until a little after six in the morning. So, you can stay here and drink, or whatever, or leave and come back. Be here a little after five so we can do this. It's not far, but the timing is pretty tight."

Jeff nodded and thought for a minute. He wanted to go home to curl up in bed with Anya and Lumpy, but then he knew that would bring up questions from Anya and he wouldn't want to get out of bed to come back here. "I'll stay here. Thanks for letting me know."

Hours later, Darius came over and shook Jeff awake in the booth where he had fallen asleep, then handed him a black knitted ski mask.

Still groggy, Jeff looked at it and asked, "Something different this time?"

Darius nodded. "Yeah, I'll explain when we're on the road. You've got about fifteen minutes to get ready.

Jeff put the mask on the table and got out of the booth, stretching to loosen up his muscles and stiff neck. Then he headed to the bathroom and came back to pick up his mask.

It was another small group, five of them this time, and Willum was driving a different SUV that Jeff had never seen before. He never asked where the cars came from—another thing he didn't want to know—but this one was nicer than the last, a more recent model with leather seats. Jeff sat next to the window in the back, watching where they were going and keeping his mouth shut.

As they got to a more industrial neighborhood, Darius spoke up. "Here's the deal. In a few minutes there will be a white delivery truck going by. When I see it, I'll let you know, so, Jeff, be ready. You need to knock it over on its side, then we open the back doors. There should be a locked cage inside, so Jeff will get out with us and open that if needed. Then we clear everything out of the back as fast as possible and get out of here. The important stuff is what's in the cage.

"Before you ask," he continued, looking at Jeff, "the driver should be okay as long as he is smart enough to be wearing his seat belt, but that's not our problem.

The delivery van is carrying drugs to several pharmacies across town, so no one will be expecting it for at least an hour, which is way more time than we need. And the sun won't be up until we're long gone. Put on your masks as soon as we stop in case the driver is conscious. Willum, you know where we're going, right?"

Willum nodded, mumbled, "Yes." As he reached an intersection with businesses on all sides, he turned the corner and pulled over to the side of the road, killing the lights.

"The van will be coming from in front of us. The only marking on it is a company name on the door, so it isn't obvious. Jeff, when I give you the word, you hit it."

Jeff nodded, then slipped on the ski mask as the rest of them did the same. He rolled down his window so he was ready when the time came.

No more than five minutes later, a small white delivery van turned onto the street at the end of the block, heading towards them. Darius, who was watching with binoculars, said, "Okay, this is it. Hit him when he gets next to us."

Jeff tracked the van and when it got about two cars away it started slowing to make a turn. He slammed it near the back top corner, tipping the van over onto the passenger side.

Except for Willum, who stayed in the driver's seat,

they all jumped out and ran to the back of the van. Jeff blew the doors open and Darius went around the front to make sure the driver wasn't going to cause them any issues.

The others were filling bags with stuff when Jeff saw the locked cage behind the driver's seat. This was where the controlled substance drugs were kept locked up even in the van. Though the driver had a key to it, Jeff wasted no time blasting the cage door open. One of the other guys jumped in and pulled everything out of the cage, throwing the bottles and boxes in his bag. It took less than two minutes to clean out the drugs, and they jumped back in their SUV.

Looking over at Jeff, Darius said, "Hit the van again so it rolls over onto its top."

Jeff did that, though it almost went all the way over onto the other side. With that, they got out of there.

CHAPTER 47

Lainie had called Jeff earlier and suggested they meet for lunch. She picked a small restaurant convenient for both of them.

Jeff arrived there first, so he got a table in the quieter back part of the room, and waited for his mother. She arrived a few minutes later, right on time. As she approached the table, he got up and kissed her cheek before she sat down.

"So, I'm assuming you wanted to talk about something?"

Lainie smiled. "Well, first, I thought I'd buy you lunch to celebrate your new job."

"I guess Anya told you about that?"

Lainie grinned at him. "Yep. Seems I talk to her more than I do to you these days, but that's okay. She's really sweet, Jeff."

He gave her a small smile. "I'm glad you two get along."

Looking at him in mock horror, she replied, "I'm not that hard to get along with, am I?"

Jeff laughed. "No. You know what I mean."

She reached across the table and put her hand over his. "I'm glad you two met. You seem like a perfect match for each other."

He nodded. "Well, we have occasional minor issues, but they're minor. Overall, things are really good between us."

A waitress came by and offered coffee, which they both declined. Then she handed them menus and left to greet another table that had been filled.

"I'm glad to hear that. Any news on Lumpy?"

"Nope. The doctor says everything looks normal, though it's getting close to time and Anya's complaining about waddling around like a duck."

"I hope you're not picking on her."

He shook his head. "No, I don't want to get her mad at me."

Lainie nodded. "Good choice." As the waitress came back, Lainie mentioned, "This one is on me today."

They both ordered the daily special, garlic shrimp linguine, and a glass of wine. The waitress took the menus and headed off to place the order.

Jeff rubbed his jaw. "I'm guessing that you had a specific reason for wanting to meet today?"

Lainie nodded, then paused while the waitress put their wine glasses on the table and left again. "Well, I do have some concerns about the other things going on in your life. What's happening in that department?"

Jeff rubbed his chin with his hand for a moment, choosing his words. "Well, not much is changing in that area. It's the same stuff every time. Nothing big or dangerous."

Lainie raised her eyebrows. "This from the guy who got shot in the shoulder?"

He shrugged. "That was a one-time thing. The recent stuff hasn't been dangerous. And besides, that guy surprised us. No one knew he lived there."

Lainie shook her head, looking down at the table and saying nothing. Then their lunches arrived, so Jeff got a brief reprieve.

Lainie took a forkful of her salad but paused before putting it in her mouth. Looking over at him she asked, "What are you doing with the money you're getting from this extra-curricular project?"

"I've been putting it in a savings account in my name. I don't want to use it and we don't need it for anything." He started fiddling with his wine glass. "It doesn't seem right to use it. I'm not doing this for the money."

"So it will go to Anya if something happens to you?"

He nodded. "Yeah, that's how the account is set up."

"Jeff, do you have any idea how much I worry about what you're involved with?"

He nodded. "Yeah, I can guess. This is not a line of work I chose, though. I'm stuck with it for being a freak."

Lainie shook her head. "I wouldn't go that far."

Jeff shrugged and took a bite of his lunch.

"Have you come up with a way to get out of this situation?"

Jeff shook his head, turning down one corner of his mouth. "I wish."

Lainie took a big drink of wine. "You know, there are other agencies that might be able to help you. Like the FBI."

He looked across the table. "Mom, don't." Shaking his head, he added, "If it was me, I'd do that in a second, but it's not. It's Anya, Lumpy, Beatriz, and maybe even you and Laura. If it gets out, we all lose. I can't risk it. Even if it could work, it would mean my abilities would be public knowledge, and that could put me at a bigger risk."

Lainie sighed, looking down at her food. "Somehow I thought you might say something like that. I'm worried about you."

He nodded. "Me too."

CHAPTER 48

Jeff was talking to Colin at the bar when Darius stormed out of the back room. Spotting Jeff, he strode over to him. Reaching into his pocket, he pulled out a set of keys and tossed them to Jeff.

"White Saturn. You're driving."

Leaving his beer on the counter Jeff headed out and spotted the car two doors up on the right. He headed that way, Darius right behind him.

"Only the two of us tonight?"

Darius nodded as he got in the passenger side.

Jeff started the car and looked over. Darius was still fuming. "Where to?"

"I don't care, drive. Get us out of here before I do something stupid."

Jeff pulled out into the light traffic and headed away towards the western part of town, saying nothing. He figured it would be best if he didn't ask questions, so he waited.

A couple of miles later, Darius spoke up. "That guy

really pisses me off sometimes. He thinks he is God and I should do whatever he wants at the drop of a hat. Doesn't even care if we can't do it. Do this, do that, and don't ask questions."

Jeff shrugged. "Is this about Captain Brady?"

Darius looked over at him with a frown. "More like Your Lordship Brady if he had his way." He stopped talking for a while as Jeff drove. "Knock something over for me."

Confused at the lack of direction, Jeff rolled down his window and looked around. Seeing a couple of trash cans waiting to be picked up, he knocked them over, dumping the contents into the street.

Sighing, Darius turned to him with an annoyed expression. "Knock yourself out next time."

Jeff glanced over but said nothing, unsure what was expected.

"Ah, forget it. I'd like to put a bullet through his fat head. He keeps pushing to get this bank job done and doesn't seem to care if we're ready or not.

"I keep telling him we don't have the alarm codes because they've changed them like they should, but he doesn't want that to stop us. I'll be damned if I'm going to break in and leave the alarm on, it's way too risky.

"If we try to do this without it, we'll likely all wind up in jail. Does he care? No, but he should. If we go down, he's going down with us." Darius shook his head. "The idiot." He went back to staring out the windshield, ignoring everything.

As they drove along, Jeff noticed a street lamp that someone had run into, leaning at an awkward angle, but still lit up. Since his window was still open, he slowed down and knocked it over so it came crashing into the street in front of them. Then he proceeded to run over the top part of the lamp and accelerated out of there as the rest of the lights on the block went out.

Darius gave him an incredulous look, then started laughing. "Yeah, that's more like it. Thanks, I feel better now."

"Is there anything you need me to do?" Jeff asked.

"No, I needed someone to talk to and you're the only one who knows we're planning to hit a bank. The guys that were with us that night you blew the vault in the abandoned bank probably know something, but they don't know the details like you do. I told them I was testing you.

"Sometimes I'll talk to my lady, but she'd probably blabber it all over town."

This was a side of Darius he hadn't seen before, and the girlfriend was news to him. Still, Jeff was at a loss as to what to say, so he kept quiet.

"Look, I need to stay away from that place for a while.

PLEASE, SISTER

There's a bar up here in the next block. Pull in there and I'll cool down with a couple of beers. His Lordship should be gone by the time we get back."

CHAPTER 49

The next morning, Jeff and Anya were both up early and sitting in the kitchen having coffee when Beatriz walked in. They said, "Hi, Mom," at the same time, then all three of them started laughing.

Jeff got up and poured his mother-in-law a mug of coffee … she drank quite a bit of it in the mornings and halfway through the afternoons. She smiled at him when he handed it to her.

"I'm glad you're both here. I want to talk to you about something important and you should both hear it at the same time."

Anya glanced over at Jeff, puffing out her lip and drawing her brows together. "Are there problems we don't know about, Mom?"

The older woman shook her head. "Yes, and no. I wanted to talk about Lumpy a little bit."

Jeff glanced back at Anya, questioningly, but she shook her head.

"Okay, what about Lumpy?" asked Anya.

Beatriz took another sip of coffee. "Well, first of all,

why don't you want to know whether it's a boy or a girl?"

Jeff jumped in. "People lived for thousands of years not knowing what gender their child would be, and it turned out okay for them. Why not wait and let it be a surprise?"

"Well, it seems to me it would be a lot easier if we knew. You're the one who doesn't want to know, right?" she asked Jeff.

"Yeah, Anya wants to, I'm the holdout." Pausing for a moment, he added, "Did you know Anya would be a girl?"

"Well, it would have been a stupid name for a boy."

Jeff chuckled and shook his head.

She continued, "Yes, I figured since I had to do all those ultrasounds, I should get as much information as possible out of them. I knew months before she got here."

Jeff shrugged, turning down one corner of his mouth. That was not the answer he had wanted.

Anya looked at her, brows furrowed again. "Mom, what do you mean 'all those ultrasounds'? You never said anything like that to me."

"Well, that brings up the other thing I wanted to talk to you about. I was waiting to see if you were going to have the same problems I did, but you've never said anything about unusual symptoms, so I guess you're not. You'd have told me, right?"

Anya blinked. "Well, sure, if I thought it was important. But remember, I haven't done this before."

Beatriz rolled her eyes. "You might be able to hide having sex, but you sure can't hide having a child."

"Why would I even hide having sex?"

"I guess I brought you up too well. You wouldn't. You talk to me about all sorts of things, sometimes ones that surprise me. I guess I should be glad."

"Yeah, well let's go back to 'all those ultrasounds'," persisted Anya.

Beatriz finished the coffee in her mug and got up to pour herself a fresh one before answering. "When I was carrying you, there were times I would have pains that I couldn't explain. It started after about two months and continued off and on until you were born. When I mentioned it to my doctor, she wanted to do some ultrasounds to make sure there were no problems, so she did, several times, but she never found any issues, and you turned out fine."

"Well I'm not having anything like that. What were they like?"

Beatriz sighed. "I shouldn't have brought it up."

Anya looked at her, waiting.

"Oh, okay. There were sharp pains that popped up out of nowhere. Everything might be fine for weeks, then I'd get these pains for a few days and they would go away again. It wasn't like labor pains. They were sharp pains in my abdomen that lasted about ten seconds or so and then stopped. I had forgotten about them until about a month ago, so I thought I should say something."

Anya looked over at Jeff again and shrugged. Turning back to her mom, she added, "Well I've had nothing like that. I feel like I have to go to the bathroom too often and now I'm waddling like a duck. Sometimes I think I'll start quacking."

Beatriz grinned at her daughter. "Those are completely normal symptoms. It's a part of this whole pregnancy thing."

"So, do you think I'm likely to have those pains too?"

Beatriz shook her head. "No. It would have started months ago if you were like me. Like I said, I shouldn't have brought it up. I don't want you to worry about it. But if you notice anything that seems odd, come talk to me, okay?"

Anya grinned. 'Well, Jeff seems a little odd, but he's always been like that."

CHAPTER 50

The following Friday night, when Jeff pulled up to the Pigeonhole, Willum was standing outside. "Hey, the boss is looking for you and he's impatient. Grab a beer and head into the back room … secret meeting."

Jeff glanced at his watch. He was earlier than usual, but said nothing. Colin saw him coming in the door and set a beer on the counter for him. Jeff grabbed it and nodded to him, then went with Willum into the back.

"You finally made it!" exclaimed Darius.

Rather than argue, Jeff raised one eyebrow and pulled up a chair at the table.

"So here's the deal," continued Darius, "you five are the ones for the next project, which is tonight. We'll leave here a little before midnight, that's when the police change shifts, so there shouldn't be any patrols around."

Looking over at Jeff, "We finally got the codes we need. It took our hacker a while to break though, but he's verified that they work, so we're good to go.

218

"For the others here, all we need are sacks. Willum is driving and we've got an SUV big enough for all of you. I'll lead you over in the pickup I've been driving lately, so I'll be with you the whole time. This job is about four miles away so travel time will be short at that time of night, but drive carefully, we don't want to raise any suspicions.

"After the job, we come back here to the back lot and I'll take the stuff and hide it. This should be a good one for us if things go the way I've got it planned out. Any questions?"

One of the guys spoke up. Jeff recognized him but didn't remember his name. "So what are we carrying? Do we need anything special?"

Darius shook his head. "Nothing special, we'll be carrying cash, hopefully lots of it. I'll split it up and get it out to you the following week. Anything else?"

He looked over at Jeff who shook his head. No one else spoke up.

"Okay, I want all of you ready to go at 11:30. Don't get too drunk or you're off the team. You've got a couple of hours but I don't want anybody leaving here before we go. Got it?"

Everyone nodded and headed back to the bar for another beer. One of them pulled out a deck of cards and returned to the back room to play poker.

Jeff grabbed an empty booth in the corner and sat

down. Willum slid into the seat across from him to talk. "So, any idea where we're going tonight?" he asked.

Jeff shrugged, "No. I know about as much as you do. I think I know what's going down, but none of the specifics."

Willum thought for a moment. "With that talk of cash, it sounds like we're hitting a bank."

Jeff shrugged again. "We'll know in a couple of hours."

Darius came over and sat down next to Willum where he could watch Jeff. "You ready to do this?"

"As ready as I'll ever be," responded Jeff.

"I'll be driving the second car in case you have problems like the last time we tried this. You were a mess for a while after that one. If it happens again, I'll get you out of there."

Nodding, Jeff mumbled, "Thanks."

Thinking back, he remembered a lot of problems after he blew the last vault. He'd been barely able to get back to the car and Darius had dragged him halfway out. His headache hadn't cleared until around noon the next day. He sipped his beer, hoping it would be easier this time.

Three hours later, the group was hyped up and ready

to go.

"Okay, one thing I didn't mention before. When we get back here, I want both of the cars we're using taken somewhere and torched. Take them to two different places to confuse the issue. If we need them, there are spare cars in the back lot. Keys are under the passenger side mat, as usual. Anything else?"

No one had questions.

"Jeff, I'll need you to blow out a couple of security cameras *before* we get out of the cars. I'll point them out."

Jeff nodded and they all climbed in the SUV, with Darius in an old, rusty Ford pickup truck leading the way.

They drove about fifteen minutes and Darius pulled into a parking lot at a small bank in one of the more upscale neighborhoods. All of them had on gloves and ski masks as Darius had directed.

Jeff saw the first camera and blew it off the wall without even being asked. Darius gave him a thumbs-up and pointed out two more, so Jeff did those also. Then everyone except Willum climbed out and waited for Jeff to blow the back door, which only took a few seconds.

As they entered the bank, Darius punched a code into the security console, which beeped to acknowledge the entry. Then he waved Jeff over to the counter where the tellers worked and pointed to two other guys, bringing them over.

Without saying a word, Darius jumped the counter with Jeff right behind him. Darius pointed to two small vaults under the counter which served the tellers, and Jeff blew the doors off them. Darius pointed the two guys to those, then he and Jeff went to the main vault.

Jeff braced himself against a wall about fifteen feet away from the door and Darius waved everyone else away. The first try shook the vault door, but did nothing else. Summoning all his strength, Jeff slammed it as hard as he could and the door crashed backwards into the vault, filling the entire room with dust so it was impossible to see.

When it cleared a little, Jeff heard Darius send the other two guys into the big vault and saw him look around. Through the dust, Darius made his way over and bent down, grabbing him. Jeff was lifted onto the gang leader's shoulders then carried out and stuffed into the pickup truck.

CHAPTER 51

As he turned onto the street where they lived, Jeff turned off the headlights of the car and drove the remaining two blocks in darkness, as he often did. He didn't want the neighbors questioning his weekend late hours.

He pulled into the driveway and quietly closed the car door behind him, then staggered to the door. The first time he tried to unlock it, he missed the keyhole, but then the door opened.

Anya looked at him briefly then put her arm around him and helped him into the house. "How bad is it?"

"Pretty bad, but it will go away. What are you doing up, sitting here in the dark?"

"I knew something was wrong, so I couldn't sleep. Come on, I'll help you up the stairs."

Together they climbed, Jeff holding the rail with one hand and Anya with his other. They went one step at a time, which was about all that he could manage.

"Let's get you into the shower, then into bed. Do you need any drugs?"

He nodded. "A couple of ibuprofen will help. Probably help me sleep, too."

Anya handed him those and a glass of water, then took his clothes off.

"I'm not sure I can do this now. Can it wait until morning?"

"No, you're a mess and I want to make sure you're not bleeding anywhere. I'm coming in with you and I'll help." With that, she took off her bathrobe and pajamas and adjusted the water until it was warm, then helped him in.

"I can do this myself, as long as I don't fall over."

She shook her head. "Forget it, I haven't done this before, it will be fun for me. Who knows, you might even like it." She then started washing him as he leaned against the wall. Part way through, she stopped, noticing his erection. "Well, you can't be feeling too bad."

Jeff chuckled, but even doing that made his headache worse. When they finished, Anya dried them both off and took him into the bedroom, but he stopped before falling into bed and put his hands on her swollen stomach, then smiled at her and kissed her soft lips.

She laid him on his back and climbed in next to him, then reached down and started stroking him.

"Anya, I have a massive headache."

She rolled on top of him and slid him inside of her, then said, "It's been a while since we did this. Hush, all you have to do is lay there."

He winced, then grinned at her. "I thought that was supposed to be my line."

CHAPTER 52

The following Friday, Jeff got to the Pigeonhole at eight and returned home at nine, surprising Anya.

"What's wrong?" Anya asked.

He shook his head. "Nothing. There was a major party going on down there since Darius was handing out envelopes full of cash to everyone. He gave me one that was bulging and told me not to deposit it all at once or it might cause suspicion. Then he told me to get out of there, since he knew I wasn't going to party with them."

"Wow, so you have the night off?"

"Next week, too. Apparently, we got a lot of cash from the bank. He told us all to take next Friday off and come back the following one." Pausing for a moment, he added, "This would be a good time to have the baby …. you want to do that tomorrow?"

Anya smirked. "It doesn't work like that."

Jeff snickered. "Oh, well. But we could go somewhere for a few days, or even a week, if you want."

"Can you get time off from your real job?"

"Should be able to. I have about three weeks of vacation time built up, but I'll need to clear it with Steven on Monday."

"Well, I wouldn't want to go too far away in case Lumpy decides to come a few weeks early. Anyway, I sure can't see myself lying on the shore somewhere in this condition. People might think I'm a beached whale."

Jeff pursed his lips, frowning. "Anya, you look beautiful in this condition. In fact, you look beautiful all the time."

She grinned at him. "You're prejudiced."

"No, I'm in love. I love both of you."

Anya rolled her eyes. "Okay, enough of this. Let's get back to the going somewhere discussion."

"Did you have something in mind?"

"Maybe. What would you think of going out to meet your Uncle Louie if he would be agreeable? Maybe we could spend a few days there."

Jeff laughed.

"What?" Anya asked.

"I talked to Mom this afternoon. Uncle Louie left for two weeks in Florida. He has a new girlfriend and wants to impress her. So, the house is empty and he wants someone to go by and check on it a couple of times."

Anya laughed, too. "Do you think he would mind us using his house for a while?"

"Not at all. He has always told Mom and us kids we could come by anytime and stay for a while. I'll double check with Mom, but it should be fine."

Pausing, Anya frowned. "You're not thinking of bringing guns along, are you?"

"Hmm. Probably, for safety's sake. I won't make you go shooting again, you're better at it than I am already."

"What do you mean, for safety's sake?"

Jeff shrugged. "It is pretty isolated out there, so he always keeps a loaded gun around the house. Usually a shotgun, but I don't even want to try to use that. My shoulder is still a little tender from when I got shot a while back."

"Shouldn't that be all healed by now?"

"It is, mostly, but I feel a twinge once in a while. The last thing I want to do is put the butt of a shotgun against it and pull the trigger. That doesn't seem like a good idea at all. Give me a few more months and I'd be willing to try it, but not yet."

"So, what do you think of my idea?"

"Sounds like fun, and peaceful, too. Plus, it's still

warm enough to go swimming if we want and you won't have to worry about a swimsuit."

Anya pursed her lips. "You are incorrigible."

CHAPTER 53

As she rolled off of him onto the large beach towel, Anya murmured, "That was nice. This whole trip is wonderful. I love it out here at the farm."

Jeff grinned at her. "Yeah, kind of like a normal couple."

She smiled. "Yeah, that's true. For a few days more, we can forget about the rest of the world and let it go its merry way without us. I wish it could stay this way all the time."

Jeff nodded, then got up and waded out into the pond before he dove in to rinse off. Anya watched him for a few moments before joining him.

As they lay back down on the beach towel, Jeff asked, "Do you want to go out for dinner tonight or should I put something on the grill?"

"Let's go out. You've been doing a lot of grilling on this trip … I'm guessing you'd like a break."

"Either way is fine with me. We can go to the expensive restaurant in town if you want. Don't get your hopes too high. It's still cheaper than a normal restaurant in the city, but the food is pretty good. Heck, I might even have a glass of wine."

She smiled at him. "To rub it in, right?"

He turned down the corner of his mouth. "No. If you object, I won't."

"It's okay, I'm teasing. I told you before you don't have to stop drinking just because I can't."

"It's a plan. Dinner tonight at the finest restaurant the town has to offer."

Anya nodded, then paused. "I love you so much. I'm afraid I'd forgotten some of that with all the problems that have been following us around."

He rolled over on his side and placed a hand behind her head. Pulling her close, he then kissed her lips, not pressing for more, but holding it for a long time. "I love you, too, Anya. I'm so glad I found you. You're the only one I can talk to, and it's such a relief. Besides the fact that you're wonderful."

As he lay back on the blanket she said, "If I didn't know better, I'd think you want to make love again."

He shrugged. "Maybe later, if you feel like it.'

Anya propped herself on her elbow to watch him more closely. A wistful expression crossed her face. "You know, we've made love more often on this trip than any other time. It's nice."

"Yeah, it is nice. It's also the first real vacation we've had together."

"And, we have another four days to go."

She leaned over and kissed him briefly. "I could get used to this."

"Maybe we should take advantage of it while we can. I think our life is going to change pretty drastically when we have the baby."

Anya nodded. "That's true, but we'll still find time to make love. Mom will take care of Lumpy for a while if I ask her."

"You wouldn't feel strange about doing that?"

"Why would I? It's part of life. One of the better parts."

CHAPTER 54

The Friday after they got back from their trip to the farm, Jeff went down to the Pigeonhole and found most of the gang wandering around drinking beer and playing cards. They seemed restless. Then Darius came out of the back room and told them that there was no job planned for that night, but there would be next week. He was waiting for some additional information.

Sipping his beer, sitting alone in the back of the bar, Jeff's mind whirled, wondering if the next target was another bank. *That could turn out to be a disaster. The police are still trying to solve the last one but not making any progress, according to the newspapers. Trying another one so soon would really intensify the investigation.* Still, it wasn't his choice to make and he wasn't about to make waves by offering his opinion. He gulped down the last of his beer, then went home to spend the evening with Anya.

***

The following Friday evening, he pulled out of his driveway and drove the two blocks to turn towards the main road where he passed a police car going the other way. As he glanced in the rear-view mirror, he saw the flashing lights come on and the driver made a U-turn in the middle of the street, coming up behind him. Thinking the officer had gotten an emergency call, he pulled over to the side of the road to let him pass. Instead, the car pulled over directly in front of Jeff's car.

Stunned, Jeff rolled down the window and shut off his engine. *Could they have found some evidence that led them to me? Was there something left at the bank, or witnesses?* He took a couple of deep breaths to calm himself so he at least appeared normal. He watched while the officer got out of the patrol car and drew his gun, then cautiously approached Jeff.

"Get out of the car, very slowly. Keep your hands where I can see them."

Jeff moved an inch at a time, opening the door with his left hand while holding his right up in the air.

"Stop right there," the officer shouted. Keeping the gun on Jeff the whole time, he then shifted around so he could scan the inside the car. Apparently satisfied, he said, "Okay, get out, slowly."

Jeff put his left foot out the door but jerked against the seat belt which was still fastened.

"Right hand, very slowly. Release the belt and then get out."

Jeff tried twice to release the belt before getting it the third time; his hand was shaking so badly. He finally got it loose and cautiously moved his other foot out, holding both hands in the air.

Gun still ready, the officer came up and grabbed his shirt with his other hand and yanked him from the car and spun him around. "Hands on the roof, spread your legs. One wrong move and I'll shoot."

Jeff leaned against the car. *Am I going to jail? How did they catch up with me?* He thought about throwing the guy across the street using his mind, but then he'd surely get shot, so he leaned against the car and followed instructions.

The officer patted him down. Finding nothing, he pulled out his handcuffs and jerked Jeff's arm down, cuffing his right hand then his left behind his back. He marched Jeff to his patrol car where he put him in the back seat.

Locked in, with a wire screen in front of him, he sat there waiting while the officer disappeared for a moment, then came around and got in the driver's seat. As he did, he snarled at Jeff and said, "You make one move and you're dead."

As the car pulled away, Jeff asked, "Am I under arrest?"

The patrolman glanced over his shoulder and said, "Not yet. Brady wants to see you."

CHAPTER 55

Captain Brady, their inside contact on the police department, was one of the nastiest assholes he had ever met. Jeff shuddered at the name.

What on earth does he want with me? He has easy access to Darius any time he wants, so why me? Is this cop that's driving involved with the gang activities, too? How many are there?

As he looked up, Jeff noticed that they'd turned off the highway, following the path he was planning to take to the Pigeonhole.

Is that where we're going? Why did they come and get me when I was heading that way myself? Why not wait until I got there?

He wanted to ask more questions, but thought better of it. If this patrolman wasn't part of the illegal stuff going on, asking the wrong question could be a bad move.

Better to wait. This guy is already angry and I don't want to provoke him anymore.

At least he wasn't going directly to jail.

PLEASE, SISTER

As they came up on Palmer Street, Jeff saw another police car with flashing lights blocking the road. All traffic was being turned away. By this time, his hands were wet with sweat and he shook uncontrollably. At a wave from an officer standing in the street, they drove up on the curb to get onto Palmer and pulled over a few buildings down from the intersection.

Jeff stared, frozen, into the bedlam of flashing lights, with six police cars in the street and police behind each one. Gunshots sporadically rang out both from the police and inside the Pigeonhole, which by now had all of its windows blown out. As he watched, the barrel of a shotgun poked out from one of the bar windows and fired at the police, who returned five or six shots of their own.

One of the policemen poked his head up from behind his car and fired another round into the bar. Jeff recognized him—Brady.

As the patrolman dragged him out of the back seat, Jeff saw Brady look up and motion them to a building entrance a few stores down. Bent low to stay behind the cars, Jeff was hurried over there and turned into the alcove, out of the line of direct fire. Brady rushed over and moved himself into the opening with them.

"Here's the deal," said Brady, snarling at Jeff. "We're taking this gang down and you're going to help. Don't give me any crap about it 'cause I know what you can do."

Jeff nodded, shaking, waiting to see what the Captain wanted.

"See that corner of the Pigeonhole between the two windows? I want you to blow that out. There's several of them hiding back there and I want them gone. Any questions?"

Jeff quickly glanced around the corner to see what he meant, but it was pretty clear what he was asking. "I need to get closer, and I need my hands free."

Brady slapped him across the face. "No more crap."

Jeff shook his head. "No, I have to. We're too far away and I use my hands to direct where I'm hitting."

Brady punched him in the stomach, doubling him over, but then took off the handcuffs. "You try anything and I'll put a bullet in your head."

Jeff looked again and turned back. "Can we get over behind that car, there? It's closer. Otherwise it might not work."

Brady frowned, but grabbed his arm and said, "Keep down," while rushing him behind the car Jeff had pointed out. "This is all you get. Do it or you're dead."

Jeff glanced over the hood of the car. There was a clear shot for him, but with the bullets flying around there wasn't any room to make a mistake. Holding his hands in front of him, he popped his head over the hood and blew out the corner of the bar, dropping back down afterward.

Dust poured out, hiding everything for a few moments, but as it settled he saw the corner of the bar that supported that end of the building was gone, leaving nothing but a pile of bricks. As he ducked back, a bullet grazed the hood of the car and whistled by his ear. He dropped to the ground, shaking, head throbbing, leaning back against the car, protected partially by the wheel and tire.

Brady fired off a few shots into the building then turned back to him. "Okay, now I need you to take out the part of the wall to the left where the door is. Got it?"

Jeff, his head aching, stared up at him, unable to move, and said nothing.

'Hey, did you hear me? Do the other part. Now!"

Jeff tried to get his feet under him, but then fell onto the street, dazed.

Brady grabbed him and pulled him up, slamming him back into the car. "Now, asshole, do it!"

Jeff staggered to his feet with Brady's help, then crouched down. He glanced over the hood again and pulled back. "Okay, okay, give me a second."

The only second that he got was the one it took for Brady to slam his gun into Jeff's face, leaving him lying in the street with his nose and cheek bleeding.

But there are some good people in there, too. Colin did nothing wrong except what he was forced to do. He seemed more like a friend stuck in a bad place than anything else.

Shaking his head, Jeff struggled back to his knees and turned toward the Pigeonhole. Then it hit him. He knew what he needed to do, if he could pull off one more hit.

Rising to a crouch, he glanced over again to make sure he had this right. Then he popped his head over the hood and slammed the wall and the whole lower floor of the building with everything that was left in him.

Again, there was more dust obscuring the bar, but he stayed on his feet long enough to be sure the wall was out before he slid down to the ground.

Brady grabbed him and spun him around. "No more shit from you. Do what I tell you."

Dazed, Jeff stared at him, then looked up over Brady's shoulder.

Watching the building, he saw the cracks starting above the blown-out windows of the Pigeonhole. It moved slowly at first, then, the entire front wall, all four floors of it, crumbled, arching out over the street, headed right at them.

Jeff managed a brief smile and thought, "Anya."

CHAPTER 56

Anya screamed.

Beatriz, watching television five feet away, jumped up and rushed over to the recliner. "Is it the baby?"

Anya stared out into space and said nothing.

"Anya, what's wrong? Do I need to take you to the hospital?"

Anya struggled to bring things into focus and looked at her mother, not even recognizing her. "Hospital? What?"

"Is it the baby?"

Anya moved her hands to her stomach and turned her head to face her mother. She shook her head slowly. "No. It's Jeff. He's gone."

Sucking in a deep breath, Beatriz backed up and stared at her daughter, eyes wide. "Are you sure?"

Tears seeping from her eyes, Anya said, "He's always been there. Ever since the first time we met, I knew even when we weren't together. And now, all of a sudden, he's gone."

"Oh, my God. I was afraid of this. It's like when I knew your father was gone. All at once, he disappeared and I couldn't feel him anymore."

Anya's tears were pouring out, though she made no move to wipe them off. "No! It can't be. He has to be there!" She hit her mother's arm with her fist, then stared at her as the older woman sat on the arm of the recliner and put an arm around Anya's shoulder.

"Not again. I tried to warn you. But not so soon, not with a baby on the way. God, Anya, this is terrible. I'm … I'm so sorry."

Anya said nothing, turned her head into her mother's shoulder and sobbed.

After a long while, Beatriz pulled her arm away and stumbled into the kitchen, then returned with a glass of water.

Anya looked at her in a trance, then knocked the glass out of her hand to the floor, where it shattered. "No!" She let out a wail that filled the room, thrashing in the chair. "It can't be. I won't let it!"

Ignoring the glass, Beatriz sat back on the edge of the chair and put her arm around Anya again. "I know, baby, it can't be." She brushed the hair off her daughter's forehead. "Shush, shush."

They sat there together for what seemed like hours, Anya sobbing and Beatriz weeping beside her. As Anya's sobs slowed, she looked into her mother's eyes. "It was like this with my father?"

Beatriz nodded. "Yes, I knew the instant he disappeared even though he was hundreds of miles away and I hadn't heard from him for weeks. It was like a piece of my heart was ripped out."

For a moment, Anya stared at her mother, then turned her head into the older woman's shoulder and started sobbing again.

***

A pounding on the door woke Anya. She looked around, confused about why she was sleeping in the recliner and what the noise was. Then it all came back to her.

Anya saw Beatriz hurrying down the steps, wrapping a bathrobe around herself and heading to the front door, where there was another loud knock.

Two policemen stood outside and one stepped forward to address her mother. "Ma'am, I'm sorry to wake you up this early, but we have some news for Mrs. Anya Merriwether."

Beatriz glanced over her shoulder to the recliner, where Anya sat crying. "I think you better come in."

With that, she opened the door and the officers, one male and one female, came into the house. Seeing Anya crying in the recliner, he looked at Beatriz. "Is everything okay here?"

Beatriz shook her head, then took them over to Anya, who looked at them with her nostrils flared, as if they were responsible for everything.

The female officer looked over at Anya. "Mrs. Merriwether?"

Anya nodded.

"We're here from the police department," she continued. "I'm afraid we have some bad news for you."

Anya still stared, saying nothing.

"Ma'am, it's about your husband, Jeff. I'm sorry to tell you this, but he was killed last night in the downtown area."

Anya stared at her for another moment, then wailed, "Nooo!" and curled into a ball in the recliner, sobbing and shaking.

The officer looked at her partner, then at Beatriz. "Ma'am, is there something we can do to help?"

Beatriz shook her head. "Not unless you can bring him back."

Putting her head down, she replied, "I'm sorry. I wish I could do that." After a brief pause, she asked, "Would it be possible for us to come back later? We do have some questions for Mrs. Merriwether."

Beatriz nodded to them and said, "Give us a day or

two. This will take some time."

"Yes, ma'am, we'll do that."

CHAPTER 57

Beatriz spent much of that morning on the phone, talking to Lainie, Laura, and Jeff's friends. None of his friends could believe it, though his mom and sister had their suspicions about what had gone on.

"What happened? Why was Jeff even down there that night? Who could have done this?" The same types of questions came up every time from each person. None of them could believe Jeff had enemies. The most asked question was "Why?"

The only person who reacted differently was Jeff's old boss, Dan, who expressed his condolences, saying Jeff would be missed. Dan also asked if there was anything he could do to help the family or Anya, whom he had heard about but never met.

Beatriz, comforted by that, just said, no, there wasn't anything he could do. Dan said he would at least take care of things in the HR department for them so Anya could get everything she was entitled to. Beatriz thanked him and told him she would let him know when the arrangements were made.

Around noon, Lainie showed up with a tear-stained face and enough food for a dozen people. She gave hugs to Beatriz and Anya, who was still silent, weeping off and on. No sooner had she done that than the bell rang again. This time it was Laura.

After a brief, light lunch during which Anya nibbled on a sandwich but nothing else, they moved into the living room to talk.

The morning papers had talked about a gunfight on Palmer Street between a notorious gang and the police. But the press expressed wonder over the fact that many of the people killed, four police and eight civilians, were killed by the collapse of the building. Another twelve gang members had died of gunshot wounds. The only survivors were four police who were beyond the range of the collapsing wall and one civilian found later who had crawled under the massive wooden bar in the tavern when the building started collapsing. The police department had no comment other than to express sorrow for the lives of the brave officers who had perished.

Lainie looked first at Beatriz, then Anya. "Do either of you have any more information about what went on last night?"

Beatriz shook her head. "Jeff didn't mention anything out of the ordinary when he left here. Did he say anything to you, Anya?"

Pulling herself out of the vacuum she was in, Anya mumbled, "As far as I knew it was like any other Friday night. Nothing special."

"Any ideas about the why the building collapsed?" Lainie continued, still looking at the two women.

Beatriz shook her head, but Anya started sobbing again. After a few minutes, she said, "I'm afraid Jeff did that—to protect me." She covered her face again, sobbing. After a moment, she added, "There had to be another way."

Lainie shook her head. "Knock down a building? Could he have even done that?"

Anya stopped sobbing and looked at her, comatose. "He'd blown bank vaults—it wouldn't surprise me. He'd been getting stronger the more he did it. That's what I'm afraid of, that he took down the building for me, even though it killed him, too." She started sobbing again, then curled up on the couch, leaving them to speculate.

A few minutes later, there was another knock on the door. Lainie opened it to two different police officers.

"Ma'am, I'm sorry to bother you now of all times, but we need someone to identify the body."

Lainie looked at Beatriz. "I'll go. He's my son."

I'll go with you," Beatriz said as she glanced over at Laura. "You'll stay here with Anya?"

Laura nodded.

Ten minutes after they left, the doorbell rang again.

Laura opened it to see an attractive man in a gray suit who pulled out a badge.

"Sorry to bother you. Are you Mrs. Merriwether?"

"No, I'm her sister-in-law. She is resting at the moment. Is there something I can help you with?"

He paused for a moment. "I'm Detective Thornton. It's important that I talk to Mrs. Merriwether. I have a couple of questions about her husband's involvement in the incident downtown. It should only take a few minutes."

Laura arched her left eyebrow, then opened the door further and invited him in. "Give me a minute. I'll see if she'll talk to you."

Laura walked over to the couch to talk to her sister-in-law, then motioned Thornton over to where Anya still sat, dark shadows under her eyes, scraggly red hair sticking out in all directions.

Anya stayed on one end of the couch and the detective sat at the opposite end, facing her. "I'm sorry about your loss, Mrs. Merriwether. I have a couple of questions for you about Friday night."

Anya nodded, saying nothing.

The detective pulled a small notepad from his inner jacket pocket and glanced over it for a moment. "First of all, could you explain to me why your car is in a No Parking zone on Marine Avenue, about four blocks from here?"

Anya sat up straighter, startled. "What? Why is it there? I thought Jeff took it downtown."

The detective nodded. "We looked for his car in the area around Palmer Street, but didn't find it. One of our patrolmen reported it on Marine, but we have no idea why it is there or how your husband got from there to the downtown area. Have you been having any car troubles lately?"

"No, new tires and an oil change a couple of weeks ago. It's been running fine," Anya replied flatly.

"Did he contact you any time Friday evening?"

Anya wearily shook her head. "No. He left here a little after seven and that was the last time I saw him." Tears began rolling down her face again.

"I'm sorry to put you through this at such a difficult time, but we're having some difficulty piecing things together. Would your husband have called any of his friends to take him downtown, by any chance?"

Again, Anya shook her head. "We've been in contact with all of them and nobody said anything like that. They all wondered what he was doing in the middle of all that mess. They would have said something if he had called."

"Hmm, I see. Ma'am, was it common for him to go downtown on Friday nights?"

Anya started twisting a strand of hair around her finger. "He went down there most Fridays, but I don't know exactly where or what he did there. Most times when he came home he was pretty drunk, but I didn't want to upset him by asking too many questions."

"Was he easily upset?"

"Not exactly. Sometimes he would stop talking to me for a day or two, that was all."

Thornton made a few notes on his pad, then turned back to Anya. "Ma'am, we're having a difficult time determining what caused the building to collapse in the middle of a gun fight. Did your husband have any experience with explosives?"

Anya put her head forward, eyes wide, staring at him. "What? Explosives? Jeff had a hard time getting the grill started."

"And there was nothing that he told you that might give us a clue as to what happened?"

Anya, still wide-eyed, shook her head.

Thornton put his pad away and rose from the couch. "Thank you very much for your cooperation." He handed her a business card. "If you happen to think of anything that might help us, you can reach me at that number."

Laura rose and escorted him to the door.

"Oh, by the way," Thornton added, "would you like me to give you a lift to get the car?"

Laura shook her head. "Can we leave it there for now? We'll pick it up in a couple of hours."

He nodded. "Sure, I'll call it in so they don't tow it away."

As Laura closed the door behind him, Anya saw her roll her eyes, and she realized she needed to be very careful what she said.

CHAPTER 58

The funeral service was held several days later, after Anya and Beatriz had picked out a casket and grave site. Anya recognized most of the people that showed up, but there were several she had never met.

The first person who introduced himself to her was Jeff's former boss Dan. After extending his apologies, he said that he would need to talk to her soon to get papers signed for Jeff's company insurance policy. "It isn't urgent, from our standpoint, but I'm sure you'd like to put the formalities behind you so you can focus on other things, like the baby."

Anya nodded, staring into space. "Give me a few days," she muttered.

The other person she didn't know was Jeff's Uncle Louie, who had always seemed to be away from his farm when they went there. He was a tall, thin man in his late forties with brown hair speckled with gray. "Anya, it's so nice to finally meet you. I wish it was under better circumstances. Jeff deserved so much more than this."

Anya mumbled a quiet "Thanks. It's nice to finally meet you too."

253

"By the way, when you're feeling better, feel free to come and visit any time you want to get away from things for a while. You and the baby, both. It might be good for the child to see another side of life. I know Jeff and Laura always loved to come out to the farm and run around, sometimes for hours. I want you to feel as welcome there as he did."

"You're very kind…" she stammered, at a loss for what to call him.

"Uncle Louie is fine. You and your child are part of the family and always will be."

"Thank you, Uncle Louie. Jeff and I had a good time there when we visited. It is beautiful."

Louie nodded and gave her a brief hug as Lainie came over to talk to Anya.

"Anya, how are you holding up?" Lainie asked, placing her arm around the girl.

Noticing the tear streaks on her mother-in-law's face, she said, "Apparently about the same as you are."

Lainie nodded and gave her a hug, tears starting again. "God, I miss him. I can't imagine what you're going through with a baby due in a few weeks. But remember, I'll be there for both of you as much as I can. If you need anything, let me know. I can take you to the hospital, I can babysit, I can … whatever." She broke into more tears.

Anya nodded, and quietly said, "I know, Mom."

As Anya was about to turn away, she noticed a young man with red hair standing on the other side of the grave site. Seeing her look at him, he reached out with the set of crutches that he'd been leaning on and hobbled over. It looked like he was still getting used to walking with his leg in a cast.

"I don't think we've met," Anya ventured as he got closer.

He leaned one crutch against the side of his body and extended his hand. "Colin Shanahan. You must be Anya. Jeff mentioned you once or twice when he was at the Pigeonhole."

"Oh, umm, so you worked for Darius?"

He gave her a lopsided grin. "Not out of choice. Kind of like Jeff. I owed them some money. All I ever did for them was tend bar. Jeff and I talked a few times."

Dropping the tenseness from her shoulders, Anya said, "Oh, pleased to meet you. I didn't realize there was someone else who didn't want to be there."

Colin nodded. "Yeah, you could put it that way. It was pretty much the two of us. Gambling debts, you know how that goes, so it was a way for me to get back even. I guess that debt is a thing of the past, now."

Anya cocked her head sideways and drew her eyebrows down. "What do you mean?"

Colin stood a little straighter. "As near as I can tell, I'm the only one from the gang that got out alive. Hadn't you heard that?"

Anya shook her head. "No, not really. I never had any contact with them. Is that what happened to your leg?"

"Yeah, I jumped under the bar when the walls started coming down. Guess I was lucky to only get a broken leg. And we should both be safe now. There's no one left to come after either of us. I'm sorry about Jeff. He was the only one there I liked."

She smiled. "Thanks for coming, and telling me that. I wasn't sure if they were all gone or not."

He nodded, then hobbled away as Anya watched.

CHAPTER 59

The next few weeks were a whirlwind of activity, while Anya talked to Jeff's company, neighbors and friends, and, most often, the police.

Since no one could figure out why the building fell, the police spent their time talking to the only person they thought might be able to help—Anya:

"There was no evidence of an explosion. Do you have any idea what might have triggered something like this?"

"Could Jeff have knocked down this building, somehow?"

"Tell me about your relationship with your husband, Mrs. Merriwether. Was there anything odd about his behavior?"

After a week of this, Anya was tired and angry at all the interruptions. Then Detective Thornton showed up again, asking her again about explosives.

"Leave me alone!" she shouted. "I know nothing about it. Why don't you go do your job and figure it out yourself instead of hounding me all the time? I'm fed up with this and I don't want to see you again

257

unless you have a warrant. Now get out of here!"

As she slammed the door behind him, she leaned back against it, looking around the living room. Then it dawned on her: this is exactly why Jeff had been afraid if word of his abilities got out. The police would hound him until he confessed, or possibly lock him up as a suspect in the killings. It would have been far worse for him if he had to lie to them. Instead, she was having to hide things from them. Still leaning there, she started crying again.

After that it was quiet for a week or so as Anya and the family continued to adjust to the new normal.

Until Friday morning.

Anya woke up earlier than normal and immediately called out to her mother. "Mom, the bed is wet. I think my water broke."

"Are you having contractions?" she asked as she rushed into the room.

"A few, during the night, but not a lot. I thought they were false labor like the others lately."

"How close together?" her mother asked.

"Maybe fifteen minutes. Nothing regular."

Beatriz helped her daughter out of bed and over to the bathroom. Then, as she took the sheets off the bed, she said, "I'll be right back. If you need anything call me right away."

"Okay, if I…" She suddenly stopped, holding onto the door frame as Beatriz rushed over, to help support her.

As Anya started taking deep breaths again, she looked at her Mom.

"That was a big one, huh?"

Anya nodded.

"Well, let's get you dressed."

A few minutes later, with her mother's help, Anya had managed to get dressed and sat back down on the bed.

Beatriz glanced at her watch. "Hmm, not real close yet, but I'll call the doctor's office and see what they want you to do."

Wiping the fresh sweat from her brow, Anya looked at her. "This goes on how long?"

Beatriz watched her cautiously. "Hard to know. Maybe yours will be short like mine was—about four hours."

Anya's eyes got wide. She opened her mouth to say something but another contraction took her breath away.

"Oh, my gosh, that was quick. I'm calling the doctor

right now. Stay here while I do that." Beatriz rushed out of the room and downstairs, where Anya heard her riffling through some papers, then talking on the phone. "Yes, the last ones were about three minutes apart. Okay, we're on our way."

***

Four hours later Anya delivered a healthy seven-pound, four-ounce baby boy. Exhausted and sweaty, she grinned at the child as they placed him in her arms and she kissed his forehead then moved him to her breast.

A short time after that, the doctors were gone, Lainie was still on her way over, and Beatriz had left the room for a cup of coffee. Anya, enjoying this moment of privacy, looked down at the little boy lying on her chest. "Somehow," she said, "I think you're going to turn out like your father, maybe in more ways than one. I'm going to call you Jeff, like him." She closed her eyes for a brief moment, then opened them, looked at him again, and whispered, "God help you, little one."

The End

ABOUT THE AUTHOR

Robert Crandall graduated from Washington University in Saint Louis, where he was born and lived most of his life. He worked in Information Systems before turning to fiction. Currently, he resides in a quiet western Saint Louis suburb and prefers to drink single malt Scotch.

Note from the author: Thank you for reading this book. As an independent writer, reviews can be very important, so if you enjoyed this book, please leave a review on your favorite book website. Thanks again!